HER PRINCE CHARMING BOSS

Billionaire Boss Romance

CAMI CHECKETTS

Birch River
PUBLISHING

COPYRIGHT

FREE BOOK

Sign up for Cami's VIP newsletter and receive a free ebook copy of *The Resilient One: A Billionaire Bride Pact Romance* here.

You can also receive a free copy of *Rescued by Love: Park City Firefighter Romance* by clicking here and signing up for Cami's newsletter.

CHAPTER ONE

Kit Abbott reclined the plush leather seat in Slade Steele's luxurious private jet. She'd left Slade and her best friend Mae Delaney in each other's arms outside Slade's downtown Boston office building a few hours ago.

"My work here is done," she declared to herself, and then laughed, hoping the flight attendant and pilot weren't listening to her. She was incredibly happy right now and didn't mind the world knowing it. Mae had tragically lost her entire family at fourteen, and she was the most amazing person Kit had ever known. Her friend deserved the happiness of being loved by the handsome, kind, and charming billionaire Slade Steele.

Kit's phone rang. She yanked it out, wondering if Mae was calling. The number was unknown. She almost pressed the button to silence it, but she wasn't used to being alone and didn't mind the interruption from talking to herself.

"Hello?"

"Miss Abbott?" The voice was deep and appealing. If this was a telemarketer, his company had scored hiring a man with a voice this enticing.

"Yes, my man with a deep and awesome voice, you found me."

He chuckled, and Kit had to swallow hard. His laugh was even more charming than his voice. Who was this, and how did he get her number? *Oh, my, goodness*, she had wondered if this would happen. She was already being blessed for all the extra time spent on her knees begging the good Lord to help her friend, Mae, overcome her fears and find the love of her life.

"Glad to hear you like my voice."

"Lucky for you, since it's all I know about you at this point. Who is this?"

"Colin Johanson."

Colin Johanson, Colin Johanson, her mind scrambled but came up blank. She was ninety percent certain she hadn't gone out with him ... yet. "I'm gonna have to put you on hold, Mr. Appealing Voice, while I Google you."

He laughed. "You won't find anything about me on Google, and you don't even know why I'm calling you yet."

So that's how he wanted to play it? Pretend she didn't know why he was calling? Yeah, right. "Every man calls me looking for a date, or a personal training appointment. Either way, I don't spend time alone with anyone until I know something about them. Google hasn't failed me yet."

"You're unique. I like that."

Unique? She supposed she was, but most men started with different descriptors for her—beautiful, perfect, enthralling, fit, etc. Unique? Not sure that was a compliment.

"I'm not calling for a date, or a personal training appointment."

"Okay, then, I'll have to say goodbye before it gets creepy."

He chuckled and acted like she hadn't threatened to hang up. "I've recently purchased The Fitness Bay and have been informed by the former owner that you run the gym single-handedly."

What? Joe had sold her gym and hadn't given her any warning? That was hurtful. Joe owned the property, the equipment, and the name; but the gym had been her brainchild and was her life. How could he have sold it out from under her like this?

Her heart pounded faster. She'd been flirting with her new boss. He'd seemed to take it good-naturedly, but she didn't want to be unprofessional with the person now writing her paychecks. She sat up straighter. Her classes were packed, and everyone loved her gym. This guy should be begging her for favors, not the other way around.

"Miss Abbott?"

She pushed out a sigh. "So, you're my new boss?"

"Yes, I am."

"Okay." She wasn't sure what to say. "Would you like to meet to go over ... how the gym is running? I'm sure Joe gave you all the financial reports, or you wouldn't have made the purchase."

"I don't have time to meet in person, so I wanted to get you up to speed on this call. I'll send an email as well, so don't worry if you miss anything."

He wanted to get *her* up to speed? For all she knew, this guy had never stepped foot into The Fitness Bay. She'd poured her heart and soul into that gym. Plus, she didn't *miss* things. Some men! "Don't insult my intelligence right off the bat."

He chuckled but proceeded with, "First of all, I'd like you to hire another personal trainer and at least one more fitness instructor. It's not cost effective to pay you your hourly rate for all of the classes, and we can expand the business with another qualified trainer who's willing to work nights and weekends. It's ridiculous that the gym is sitting empty most evenings when there could be classes and training going on."

Kit's mouth flapped open, but she had no response. She was a one-woman show, and she liked it that way. Her clients adored her, they were a close-knit group and wouldn't want someone else training or teaching them.

"Second—"

"No," she finally interjected. "Backing up to the first. Why would we hire someone else? My clients love me. I'm the highest-rated gym on either side of the bay."

"That's one of the reasons I purchased this boutique gym, but also because your prices are significantly lower than they should be for membership and personal training, so we're going to increase that. And, like I said, we can maximize the space use with evening classes and training appointments."

"No way!" she sputtered.

"I apologize, Miss Abbott, but I have a little more experience in running a business than you do, and I am the owner. You will implement my changes or find yourself a new job."

Kit swallowed down the anger and fear his words created. His voice was still a beautiful bass but not appealing at all anymore. *What a jerk.* She'd built her gym from the ground up. True, she wasn't the owner, because she'd been fresh out of college and intimidated by the idea of securing a loan and being financially responsible. She didn't want to rely on her parents and brothers to co-sign or give her a handout. So, she'd approached a local businessman, and he'd been great to work with her. The traitor, Joe.

Now her lack of confidence in her business abilities was coming back to bite her. This joker couldn't raise the prices. Her clients were like family to her. If someone had a baby, they hosted a baby shower at the gym and organized a schedule for bringing in meals to the new mama. If someone was going through a hard time they'd spend an hour after class chatting, and someone would bring her favorite treat or take her shopping. She loved them all and did not want to raise prices on them or bring in some stranger off the street to teach or train them, but she also didn't want to get fired on the spot and have to desert them.

"How long do I have to implement your ... demands?" Maybe not the best word to use with her boss, but it was better than the other things she could've said: unreal expectations, stupid ideas, ludicrous concepts?

"You have two weeks to hire the additional help, expand your class schedule, and increase personal training options."

"Two weeks? I live in a small town, Mr. Colin Johanson, and if you haven't noticed with all your mighty business power, unemployment nationally is at a 49-year low of 3.7 percent." Her accountant brother had just told her that number at Sunday dinner, and she was grateful she'd catalogued it in her memory banks. "It's going to be tough to find someone who needs a job, let alone one who is trained and excels in the field of exercise physiology. I will not hire less than excellence."

"Unemployment has currently rebounded and is at four percent, but I really appreciate the economics lesson." His voice had laughter in it, as if she were a stupid teenager trying to teach a college professor something. "I can give you a month. I'll be checking in, and I want to hear that you're making strides, or I will do the hiring myself."

Her neck felt hot and tight, but she didn't know what to say. He was, after all, her boss now, and he held all the cards. The money cards at least. Maybe in a month, she could find a new spot to open her own gym and secure a loan for all the equipment she needed. She had a proven track record of success. Unfortunately, her new boss had that in his computer files, so she might struggle getting the proof she needed for the loan.

She'd never seen anything like this coming. Joe had been more than fair with what he paid her for running the gym; as well as the extra money for each class she taught and a high percentage of what her personal training clients paid.

He spoke again. "I also do not want to hear about the gym being closed for any reason."

"Excuse me?"

"The gym has been closed today. I understand you can't be expected to work weekends, so I'm fine with the Monday through Friday schedule for now, but I don't want closures during weekdays. Understood?"

"Yes," she muttered. This loser could now dictate her life? She didn't like closing her gym and not being there for her clients either, but she'd made sure to contact them and they all agreed that the time matchmaking Mae and Slade was essential ... essential to her friend's happily ever after.

"You'll see, once you get some people hired, that this will actually be a great thing for you. You can take vacation and not be tied to the gym. I'll check in soon."

Then he hung up. Kit blinked and stared at her phone. It was silly to feel like her world was crashing down, but she definitely felt it. Her new boss was a class-one jack-tard and she had to either comply with his wishes and find help or somehow set up her own gym and talk her clients into moving with her. One month. Somehow flying on a private jet wasn't quite as fun after that conversation.

C olin Johanson Miller hung up the phone and walked into Sushi Sticks, the restaurant that he'd purchased a few weeks ago. He liked this restaurant, a lot, and after spending the past couple of weeks pretending to be a waiter here, he'd implemented some changes; finally telling the manager and staff who he really was: Colin Miller. He went by Colin Johanson for work sometimes, Dirk Miller when he played undercover boss. He'd stolen Dirk from the Clive Cussler novels he'd devoured as a teenager. Dirk Pitt had been his hero and part of the reason he'd enlisted in the Navy, since NUMA was a real entity thanks to Clive Cussler, but he wanted adventures like Dirk Pitt and Al Giordino had, above and beyond the opportunity to preserve marine artifacts.

He thought about this restaurant and being "undercover". It was actually easier than he'd first envisioned going incognito. People saw what they wanted to see, and most recently people saw him as Dirk Miller the waiter. Until he confessed the truth to his new employees a couple nights ago, none of them connected the dots to his real life and the hype that surrounded Colin Miller, the youngest billionaire in America, eight years ago. When Kylie Jenner broke his record, he didn't attend the party but sent a nice basket and a card, relieved to have the spotlight move on.

He smiled to himself as he replayed the conversation from earlier with his gym manager. Kit Abbott had not been thrilled with his suggestions. He felt bad threatening to fire her. He'd seen her in person, at this very sushi restaurant, and she was all fire and spice and everything nice. The cute way she'd flirted with him, a few nights ago with her friend Mae by her side and at the beginning of the phone call, made him rethink the changes he wanted to make with the gym.

No. His bottom line came before an appealing beauty and empty flirtations. She would come around to see that it was silly to not utilize the space in the evenings, and extra help would give her a chance to live her life outside the gym. He wished he could get to know her outside the boss arena as Colin, but he would have to be content with getting to know her outside the boss arena, under the guise of Dirk. He regularly bought small businesses and expanded or improved them. He'd made it a rule to spend a few weeks monitoring the business as either an employee or a customer, unbeknownst to the manager and other employees. It had worked very well for him, and sometimes he'd had the opportunity to see inside stories and help employees out, similar to the Undercover Boss TV situation. Once or twice, he'd realized his changes and expectations weren't the direction the business needed to go, but usually he was spot on.

So, he'd go to The Fitness Bay tomorrow morning as Dirk Miller, the waiter Kit might remember from the sushi restaurant, and he'd make his own assessment. Being around the beautiful and vivacious Kit would be a lot of fun. He wasn't in any danger of falling for her. He'd been raised not to believe or trust any relationship. He was too busy and driven to ever settle down, especially in a small town like Sausalito. He'd have fun teasing with her as Dirk, maybe even go on a date, but that was the extent of any romance for him. In the end he'd tell her who he was, and she'd implement his changes. The gym would be more successful, Kit Abbott would be happier than ever, and he would move on to his next town and his next purchase. It always played out that way.

CHAPTER TWO

Kit rushed into her small Waldo Point floating home. It had wooden beams and dark wood trim set against pale beige walls and lots of windows. The backside of the narrow house was double sliding glass doors that were almost always open when she was home. It led out onto a deck over the calm water of Richardson Bay. She'd inherited the floating home from her grandparents. They'd bought it as a vacation home in the late eighties and spent part of their retirement years fixing up and enjoying the house.

When they gifted it to her after college, she'd been thrilled. She adored living right on the water. Kit didn't have time to enjoy the beauty or peace of her lovely bay view tonight. She hurried to shower and dress before driving to Sushi Sticks to meet her date.

Mike was waiting for her at the exterior restaurant door, his tall, well-built frame filling the space. She'd met him a few weeks ago when her friend Mae had run smack into his table, wearing her shirt, *Bring me a Diet Coke and tell me I'm Pretty*. Mike had hit on Mae, which Kit really appreciated as it had boosted her dear friend's confidence. Mae had been en route to finally meet her dream man Slade, so Kit had happily taken Mike off her friend's hands.

"Hey." He grinned, his white teeth contrasting beautifully with his deep brown skin. He had the most appealing lips. "You look beautiful." He clasped both of her hands in his, leaned down, and gave her a soft kiss on the cheek.

Kit grinned. His lips were fall-into-them-like-cotton-candy soft yet they didn't light her up or give her any kind emotional reaction. She wouldn't be falling head over heels for this guy, but he'd been kind with Mae, and he was a great mix of flirtatious and manly. "You look pretty great yourself."

He escorted her inside, and the hostess showed them to a corner table. She picked up her menu but felt his eyes on her. Tilting her head to the side, she peeked at him over the menu. "Just can't stop staring?"

His answering grin was adorable. Maybe he could be a keeper, for a week or two. Kit dated plenty of men, and then sent them on their way. She enjoyed each interaction. Men from the city and on vacation came to her little hometown every day. There was never a shortage of somebody wanting to buy her dinner. Someday, maybe, she'd find the sparks and connection she'd always dreamed of, but not today. Yet, Mike was exactly what she needed tonight to forget about the jerk of a boss who'd bought her gym. Tonight she'd relax and enjoy the company of a handsome, kind man.

"Yes, ma'am," he said.

"Are you from the South?" she asked. She'd noticed an accent before but had been too busy helping Mae to ask.

He nodded. "Born and raised in Birmingham. I live near Atlanta now."

"That's why you haven't been around to take me on a date the past few weeks."

"It's been tough on me."

"What do you do in Atlanta?"

"I play football, for the Patriots."

"Oh, wow." Her eyebrows darted up. "You're famous, and I didn't even know it."

He chuckled. "That's all right. I don't mind anonymity or a woman who doesn't fawn over me, once in a while."

"Whew." She pursed her lips and teased him, "I might need some hip waders to get through the lake of self-appreciation in here."

He laughed louder. "Forgive me. I didn't mean to come across as over-confident but some women are drawn to football players only for the name and the fame."

"I shouldn't have teased. That would be hard."

Two waters were set down on the table, and Kit glanced up to say thank you. The words got stuck in her throat. "You!"

The too-handsome waiter she'd met with Mae arched an eyebrow. Dirk, that was it. "Happy to see you again, too."

"It's not that I'm not happy, it's just ... you were so cool and mysterious last time. You gave me your card that had nothing but your phone number on it."

"Which I hoped you'd call or text." He winked at her and those bright blue eyes of his were yanking her in faster than a guppy on a tuna hook.

"I wanted to," she admitted, "I've just been helping my friend have her happily ever after."

"Mae and Slade?" he guessed, grinning at her.

He remembered.

"Yes, sir, it was beautiful."

"Not as beautiful as you."

Warmth filled her, and she felt like she was lit up from the inside at his simple compliment. She'd been told she was beautiful so many times, you'd think it wouldn't affect her anymore. The way Dirk's deep voice caressed the words as his eyes caressed her face made her want to throw herself into his arms and see how it felt to touch him, something about him shouted he might be the one ...

A throat cleared from across the table. The warmth in her abdomen turned to burning heat in her cheeks.

"Oh, Mike, I'm sorry," she gushed out.

Mike didn't look pleased, but he was such a laidback, nice guy, he didn't look like he was about to rip Dirk's head off. He stood and offered his hand to Dirk. "Mike Kohler."

The men were both built nicely, but at probably six-six, Mike had Dirk by a few inches. Football player. That made sense.

Dirk shook his hand and nodded. "I know who you are, one of my favorite wide receivers."

"Thank you." They released hands, but Mike didn't sit down. "And you are?"

"Dirk Miller. I'm just the waiter. What can I get you to drink?" He smiled, but it felt off to Kit. Just the waiter. He didn't seem like he was "just a waiter" to Kit, and she didn't love the way he put himself or his job down. It was an honorable position, and she thought anyone who worked hard and respected themselves and their job were great. She'd dated everyone from sewer cleaners to movie stars, enjoying the differences in each.

Mike finally seemed to relax and sat back in his chair. "Water's great for me, actually. Season starts soon."

"It'll be great to watch you play again." Dirk turned his blue eyes on her and Kit sucked in a breath. Wow. He was ... splendid. "And for the lady?"

"I'll take a Diet Coke."

"Living on the edge." Dirk winked conspiratorially.

"Honoring my friend's memory. She loved Diet Coke."

Dirk chuckled. "She's fallen in love, not passed away."

Kit lifted her shoulders. "They might be one in the same."

"Aw, c'mon, don't diss on love like that. Maybe you'll fall off the ledge of love someday yourself."

"Not me. I'm too fun for one man to keep up with." She gave a little shimmy dance and Dirk laughed.

A throat cleared again, and Kit blinked back to the reality that she was on a date, with a really great guy.

"I'll go get those drinks and be back to take your order," Dirk said quickly. "Any appetizers to get started?"

Mike sort of bowed his head to her. His dark eyes much too serious.

"I'd love some edamame," Kit said quickly.

"Got it. For you?" Dirk looked to Mike.

"Shrimp tempura. Thanks."

"For sure, man. Nice to meet you." Dirk gave Kit one more appealing gaze and then strode away, so confident and in charge of the world, Kit couldn't peel her eyes from his retreating form. Why was he so tempting and perfect to her?

He disappeared through the double doors into the kitchen. Kit had the sensation of being in a hot-air balloon that suddenly lost all its propane-heated air and crashed to the ground. She blinked and focused back on her dinner date. He was looking very serious and almost, uneasy. Dang, she was not treating him right.

"So, I've got a story for you," she rushed out.

"Oh, yeah?"

"Remember my friend who ran into your table at the burger place and had on the Diet Coke shirt? Mae?"

"Of course."

"So, over the past few weeks she's fallen in love with the guy she was trying to get to that night."

"Really? That's great."

"It is." Kit started into the story and Mike laughed and asked all the right questions at the right times. When Dirk came to take their orders, she focused solely on her menu. Speaking into it, she didn't let her gaze even stray to him. Kit was afraid, if she did, she wouldn't stop looking until he disappeared into the kitchen again, and she'd offend Mike even worse. Mike was so great. She didn't want to be rude to him.

Dirk brought their appetizers, and then their food with nary a word besides, "You're welcome". Kit fought diligently to keep her eyes off of the charming waiter. She let herself slip once, and it almost took her down when he pumped his eyebrows slightly and gave her a knowing smirk. He was obviously used to women clamoring at his toes. She appreciated confidence, but this guy took that appealing self-assurance to the level of, I'm-so-hot-no-woman-has-ever-turned-me-down. She looked away quickly, thinking to herself her friend Mae had turned him down for Slade. Kit could do the same for Mike, at least until the date was over.

The sushi was superb, as always. Kit loved the roll that had cilantro wrapped into it. She could never remember which raw fish she preferred, Mae always ordered for them when they came here, but it was easy to remember cilantro.

After dinner, she and Mike chatted and waited for the bill, and waited, and waited. Kit started fuming. Was Dirk making them wait on purpose? But what purpose would that serve? More time for Kit to enjoy talking with Mike didn't seem to be a very desirable idea, if Dirk was actually interested in her. He was probably just the type to flirt only to prove that he could get any woman and inflate his already massive ego.

She finally had no choice but to excuse herself to use the ladies' room. She finished and exited the room into the secluded hallway just as Dirk sauntered confidently into the space. His face lit up, and he walked right up to her. He was far too handsome for anybody's good with his dark hair and coloring and startling blue eyes. Kit backed away, repeating over and over again in her mind, *I'm on a date, I'm on a date.*

She bumped into the wall and Dirk grinned as he rested one hand against the wall close to her head and leaned in. "I knew you'd find a way to get me alone," he murmured, his eyes tracing over her face and lingering on her lips.

Panting for air from his simple glance, she realized no man had ever gotten under her skin like this one did. She was always the one in control and calling the shots. How did this man have the power to make her want only him, and how was she going to keep herself from falling for him?

"I'm on a date," she burst out. Her face flared. She was always the witty, cool one. She knew Dirk had come on to Mae the night she was supposed to meet Slade the first time, so it wasn't like she was anything special to him. A guy like this? No woman was anything special to him. He flirted, had his fun, and moved on.

Dirk nodded, his eyes solely focused on her. The bright blue of those eyes was fabulous, and she was drawn toward him, so much that she found herself leaning.

"Mike Kohler is a beast on the football field and an absolute stud, but he's not the guy for you."

"Excuse me?" She tried for righteous indignation and forced herself to push her shoulders back into the wall so she didn't gravitate toward him without conscious thought. "I'll decide who the guy for me is."

"I'm sure you will." He gave her a crooked grin that was completely irresistible. "I hope when you make that decision, you'll remember this moment." He leaned down and before she could move, protest, or fully process what was happening, his lips met hers. The kiss was tender and achingly sweet, and her lips tingled in response. Hovering just over her lips, he whispered, "Call me."

Then he straightened and stepped back out of her reach, pivoted, and sauntered toward the main part of the restaurant.

Kit was still gasping for air, but she managed to fling at him, "What if I don't call you?"

Dirk turned back, and his cheeks crinkled in an appealing grin. "You will." Then he disappeared.

Kit leaned heavily against the wall, gasping for air. She'd kissed many a man, but Dirk's kiss had been so sweet and filled with an ache of longing that she would've never seen coming from him. If he would've kissed her all demanding and passionate, she could've slapped him or dismissed him. As it was, she wasn't sure how to deal with all the emotion and desire he evoked in her. Trying to push it from her mind, she squared her shoulders and headed out to finish her date with Mike. The sad thing was, Dirk was right—Mike was an absolute stud, but it was more than obvious with the way she'd reacted to Dirk that Mike wasn't the right guy for her.

CHAPTER THREE

Dirk left the restaurant before Mike and Kit did. His employees were doing a great job and knew he was the owner now. He kept showing up to eat at Sushi Sticks and wait tables because it was fun, and he didn't like downtime. He had his evenings free and would be staying in Sausalito a little longer than he'd planned, so he could check out the gym he'd bought and see if Kit was following his advice to hire the extra help he'd demanded, as well as raising prices.

He went to his hotel at Cavallo Point. It was spacious and had great views of the Golden Gate Bridge and the greenery of Sausalito. He really liked this little spot. Smiling to himself, he grabbed his laptop and tapped out an email to Kit as Colin Johanson, instructing her on the price increases he wanted her to implement at the gym, effective July first, two weeks from now. She wouldn't like it, but her prices were far too low. Eventually she'd thank him.

He stood on the balcony of his room and looked across the bay at the lights of San Francisco. Kit Abbott. The memory of his lips caressing hers was more inspiring than this beautiful view, really than any view he'd ever glimpsed, and he'd traveled the world.

What had he been thinking? He didn't get involved with women, especially not with an employee. If she ever connected the dots between Dirk Miller and Colin Johanson, she would be royally ticked off and there would be no more sweet kisses from her. That shouldn't matter to him, but her kiss had been as intoxicating as any alcoholic drink his buddies used to force on him back in college. He didn't drink anymore, because he didn't like to have his senses muddled.

Senses muddled. That's what Kit Abbott had the power to do to him, to any man. He shouldn't have flirted with her in front of her date, Mike Kohler of all people, or outside the bathroom, and he definitely shouldn't have kissed her. Not that he was worried about breaking her heart. Kit was the type of woman that every man groveled for, it was written all over her that she was confident and used to calling the shots. He doubted his kiss had affected her much at all, and he never stayed in one spot long enough to develop anything past a shallow relationship. Plus, his parents had taught him well not to trust or love.

Yet as he had these thoughts, he kept waiting and waiting for his phone to ring. She'd never said she would call him, but he'd be very surprised if she didn't.

His phone rang. He pulled it out quickly and then groaned. His dad. "Sir," he greeted him.

"Son, where are you tonight?" The question was soft, as if his dad actually cared. Colin scoffed at the very idea. There had been many times as a child, teenager, and even young adult when he assumed his dad truly loved him and was proud of him, but those times had become few and far between after Colin's favorite stepmom died and Colin returned from the Navy. Colin was an adult and didn't need a relationship with his father. His dad jumped from one marriage to the next, spending his time trying to make each new wife feel special. Truly, neither he nor his dad knew anything about deeply caring for another person.

"Sausalito, across the bay from San Francisco."

"Beautiful spot." His dad took a breath then rushed right into it. "The sushi restaurant was a good acquisition, but I feel like this gym is a waste of time. It's too small, not enough profit margins."

Colin simply smiled. His dad liked to talk business with him, but they both knew Thomas Miller didn't make the decisions, Colin did. His dad was on the board of directors for Miller International, but the company had been passed down to Colin upon his grandfather's death. Colin owned fifty-one percent and was the president of the company. His dad was very supportive and always "so proud". Thomas was also vice-president and Colin wondered if it drove his father insane the way he ran the business, but their billions of dollars kept growing and everyone said they were pleased. Colin only flew into L.A. once a month to meet with the board, but he stayed on top of everything through email and video chats; so maybe his dad griped to the board members behind his back, Colin didn't know or care. He actually doubted his dad would say a bad word about him to anyone. Their lack of a substantial relationship was Colin's choice. His father tried hard, Colin could be man enough to acknowledge that.

"Aren't you getting tired of these onesie, twosie businesses, changing towns all the time? I'd love for you to settle down, live close to Tracy and me."

Colin bristled. He hated when his dad chided him to "settle down". What did his father know about settling down? "You get enjoyment out of tennis and Tracy for a few more months. I'll get my enjoyment from playing undercover boss and helping out small businesses until I tire of it."

Silence fell on the line. His dad didn't appreciate him dissing on his wife of the moment and whatever hobby each new wife wanted him to excel at. Colin supposed he should be grateful his dad's moral compass was strong enough that he always divorced the last wife and married the new one before becoming intimate, but it was still tough to keep up with the string of beautiful, younger women in his dad's life. He thought Tracy was wife number seven, no, it was definitely eight. He was pretty certain Tracy was closer to his age than his dad's, but "age doesn't matter in the eyes of the good Lord and when it comes to true love". He rolled his eyes. The woman actually had the gall to say that to him when Colin graciously made an appearance at their ostentatious wedding.

"Colin," his dad's voice dropped lower, and Colin cringed. Apparently, it was time for emotional instruction instead of business. "I know your mom and Melanie both did a number on you. Me too, son. Me too."

Colin squeezed his eyes shut. He hated being called son. Worse, he hated hearing about his mother. Yet even worse than that was his dad daring to bring up Melanie. The woman they'd both fallen in love with after Colin's mom left them. The only woman Colin had actually connected with and to, his mother figure and closest friend throughout his teenage and early young adult years.

"But someday you need to choose to forgive, move on, and find love. All this traveling, all these small businesses. I admire what you do, son, helping the employees and being on the nitty gritty end of the business. Everyone loves you, the board sings your praises. You're insanely wealthy, successful, charming, handsome, but you turn thirty this year, Colin. Don't you think it's time to let love into your heart and settle down?"

"No, sir." He kept it short. It was the only way. If he mocked love or argued about any of his dad's points, Colin would be in for an hour-long "discussion". Was it still considered discussion if it was all a lecture? And who was his dad to give him advice on settling down? The man who married and divorced faster than Henry VIII? At least his dad didn't behead his wives. Just gave them a nice alimony package, a pat on the rear, and said goodbye.

"Tracy's got me going to her church. We'd love to have you come sometime."

His dad's change of tactic was surprising, and foreign. As far as he knew his dad had never stepped foot in a church. He knew he personally hadn't. He wasn't interested in discussing it. "Thanks for calling, Dad. Good luck with tennis." He almost mocked the church thing, but he had enough respect for whoever orchestrated things above to not go there.

"Goodnight, son." His dad's voice was heavy and sad.

Colin shook off the conversation and the frustration it created. His mom had ditched them both when Colin was eight, and then she'd gotten arrested for dealing drugs. He had no clue where she was now and told himself often that he didn't care. His favorite stepmom, Melanie, was gone too, but Colin never let himself think about her demise or his father's hand in it. No reason to fester in the anger against his father.

As the late night wore on, he focused on work requests and emails he needed to respond to. He didn't let the frustration of his now-silent phone settle in his gut. Tomorrow he'd spend more time with Kit as he evaluated her gym, and by tomorrow night she'd be the one pursuing him. It was all in the fun of the chase, but for some reason the lingering impression of her lips made him afraid that it wasn't about fun or chasing with Kit. No. He'd never follow his father's patterns. Flirting and a date or two were the end of his romantic illusions.

CHAPTER FOUR

K it started the day with a five a.m. class. All her classes were boot-camp and circuit style. She pushed the participants as hard as they'd go, while still being safe. She was big on executing lifts properly and not rushing through them, but when it was time for sprints or plyometrics, she made sure, as fast as their body could handle was her participant's speed. She also coordinated each week's schedule to maximize muscle tear down and recovery for each major muscle group, ensuring a well-rounded fitness level and decreasing chances of injury.

Her classes were mostly women. Occasionally a man came in, even more rarely a man stuck with it. Maybe it was being in a class filled with women, or perhaps the emphasis was too slanted toward cardio in balance with strength training, but men rarely stuck it out.

As the six o'clock class filtered in, she was still saying goodbye to the five a.m. participants, but Kit made sure to say hello to everyone sluggishly coming for the early morning workout. Behind the petite friends Mary and Ginger, a large figure appeared. Taken aback, Kit blinked, and then her eyes widened.

"Dirk Miller?" she burst out.

"Hey." He raised a hand and sauntered over to her. "I want to sign up for classes."

How did he look this fabulous at six a.m.? Kit self-consciously straightened her ponytail and blotted the sweat on her brow from the last class with the back of her hand. Hopefully her antiperspirant and deodorant was working.

"First class is free. If you're tough enough to come back, we'll get you signed up then." She gave him a sassy wink.

He chuckled and folded his arms across his chest. The two times she'd seen him, he'd been in a white, button down, long-sleeved shirt and black slacks. He'd looked fabulous, and it had been obvious he was nicely-built, but in a fitted grey t-shirt, he was giving her heart palpitations. His lean arms had bulges and striations in all the right spots on his biceps and triceps, and his shoulders and chest were proportioned and nicely-rounded. "Here's hoping I'm tough enough." He inclined his chin to her and went to find an open spot.

"Let's warm up," Kit called out, her cheeks flaming red. Why had he come here? Had he known this was where she worked? It had been all she could do last night to not dial his number and flirt some more, but hot shame and delicious desire warred within her when she thought of his tender kiss. She'd kissed Dirk while on a date with someone else. Kit dated a lot, but she had rules to make sure no one got hurt beyond the normal hurt of her saying goodbye, which she always did. Kissing Dirk last night broke about a dozen of those rules and made her wonder if she'd ever say goodbye to him. If he wanted to date her, that is.

Kit tried to focus on starting the class, but questions and a craving to touch him again were racing through her. She'd given her self-control a workout not calling or texting him last night, and now he was in her gym.

As the participants worked through inch-worms, squats, lunges with a twist, planks, and a half-dozen other warm-up moves, Kit's gaze kept straying to him like her eyes had a mind of their own. Down in the plank position, Dirk's arms rippled with muscle, and she found her mouth falling open. Unfortunately, he glanced up, catching her gaze and gave her a knowing smirk.

She gritted her teeth, looked away, and barked out, "Twenty pushups." Walking around the room, she monitored form and encouraged. "Mary, get those abs in. Brandi, you're killing me friend, you can go lower than that. Sarah, get off of your knees, you're too tough for girl pushups." When she reached Dirk, the ground seemed to sway. Watching that man doing pushups was like appreciating a beautiful painting.

"How's my form, boss?" he asked, grinning at her.

"Perfect," she admitted. "Military?"

"Put me through college."

He didn't even seem out of breath as he kept pumping out pushups and responding to her.

"What did you graduate in?"

"Business."

Business? That didn't seem to fit his current job, but it fit his in-charge, confident personality. "Where?"

"Harvard."

What the what? Harvard! No wonder he'd needed the military to get him through. He must be brilliant. Who goes to Harvard then becomes a waiter? "And now you're the rocking the restaurant scene as a waiter."

"Best job in the world." He finished the pushups and leapt to his feet. She was five-eight, so not short by any means, but Dirk's manly build and six-three made her feel dainty and feminine.

So, he'd graduated in business, and then come to Sausalito to be a waiter? Maybe he was a struggling artist or writer. Sausalito was famous for that. But then why the business focus? Harvard. Seriously? She had so many questions for him.

He stood, sweat glistening on his brow, and his pectoral muscles were all pumped up from the pushups. She recognized it was her fault for calling out pushups, but sheesh, did he have to wear such a tight shirt?

He leaned in closer and she found herself arching toward him. "The class probably needs their next exercise," he murmured in a deep, sexy voice.

Kit startled. His voice was ultra-appealing but something about it also gave her anxiety. She didn't have time to dwell on it as she glanced around and realized everyone was staring. A lot of her workout friends were grinning or looking much too interested in her and Dirk's conversation.

She clapped her hands. "Stations are ready and the workout's on the board. Four to five per station. Get in position." Everyone scrambled to stations, except for Dirk who stayed right in her space and stared at her.

"Where should I start?" he asked.

"Burpees." Most of her class considered burpees torture, but he could handle it.

"Where?" he asked again.

Kit reached out and wrapped her fingers around his forearm to direct him toward the burpee station. The connection of their flesh sent warm tingles through her. He startled and stared intently at her. Kit yanked her hand back and pointed, but realizing her hand was trembling, she forced out, "Over there."

He didn't give her his knowing smirk, though he had to know how affected she was by him. Instead his eyes went soft and lingered on her face. Was he feeling the same connection she was? Had he also spent last night remembering and dissecting that kiss?

Kit shook it off and barked out, "Begin!"

Dirk had to give it to her. Kit knew her stuff, and she organized a killer workout. He chatted with the ladies in his group, as much as they could for lack of oxygen, and they explained that Kit was the best trainer on either side of the bay and that her workouts were all organized to maximize their fitness levels.

His gaze kept straying to her, but that was natural for a man to have his eyes drawn to a gorgeous woman, right? It didn't have anything to do with the fact that her fingers on him had sparked a different desire than he'd ever felt before. It was a desire to kiss and hold her, but also a desire to snuggle before a warm fire and stay close to the same woman for the rest of his life. That was crazy thinking. He'd never make a lasting commitment like that. Yet he'd felt something even more intriguing and appealing than her simple touch of a few minutes ago when they kissed last night.

Ignoring these foreign feelings, he pushed himself to go faster and harder. The weighted balls they had only went up to fifty, not heavy enough to really challenge him in wall balls, so he tried to do more reps on each round. He really liked the tug-rope challenge she'd set up: a thick, weighted rope on a cable machine they had to tow as the weights on the machine rose. When Dirk got it to clank to the top, it rang like the bell of a high striker game at a carnival. The women in his group cheered when he made it ring while loaded with the maximum weight.

Sweat poured off of Dirk, and he hoped he wouldn't stink after the workout, because he really wanted more time to tease and talk with Kit. Maybe he could initiate the touch this time and see if he felt something incredible again. Nothing about his reaction to her was smart or rational, and that worried him. What if he was like his dad who fell in love at the smile and touch of any pretty woman? He'd always assumed he took after his mom, cold and unemotional. It was another reason he would never get involved and hurt someone the way his mom had hurt him.

But Kit was incredible. Watching her stride around encouraging, instructing, and modeling correct form drew him to her even more. He'd made a smart move purchasing this gym, no matter that his dad was right about the smaller profit margins. Yet he recognized what Kit had been saying about how hard it would be to hire someone with her expertise and passion for not only fitness, but for the people in the class. It was obvious they were her friends, and she was giving her all to help them be healthy and fit.

Class wound down and everyone cheered for themselves and each other. Dirk smiled. The cheering was cute, and he liked the cheesy feeling of camaraderie with these women. The last time he'd felt such fellowship had been in the military. His bond with his Navy SEAL brothers was unbreakable and deep, but almost eight years had passed since his grandfather died, and Dirk had walked away from the military to run his business.

He shook off the nostalgia of thinking of men he'd lost to death and men he'd simply lost track of and grinned at the women in his group. A few had tried to hit on him, but most treated him like a workout buddy, and they all deserved to cheer and feel accomplished for making it through that workout.

Dirk bid farewell to his group and waited for an opening to talk to Kit. The class was dwindling. but there was a new group already filtering in. Shoot. He'd hoped for some time alone to ... scope out more details about the gym. That had to be his focus. He only let emotion enter into the equation when he discovered a real-life, sad story that he could help fix. That happened often in his acquisitions and travels, and then he became the benevolent boss and the hero. The hero role was familiar because of his time with the Navy, especially when he'd been deployed in Afghanistan and Kuwait after college graduation. He'd gone the military route because his dad and grandfather didn't believe in handouts and expected him to put himself through college. The boss role was familiar as he'd been trained from childhood to be successful, driven, and in charge. This role of wanting to touch and get closer to a woman was completely foreign. Though he'd been flirted with by many a beautiful employee, attraction and connection had never factored into the equation for him.

Kit started toward him, and his heart beat harder than it had during the one-minute sets of burpees. "Hey," she said when she reached him.

She was model gorgeous with her long, blonde hair, tanned skin, teal blue eyes, and perfectly fit body, but Kit's appeal went deeper than that. He loved the way she teased with him and the spice in her. He admired the tough love she showed her class. There was also a light in her eyes that she shared with her friend, Mae, who he'd met at the sushi restaurant. Maybe a belief in a higher power? Interesting. He wanted to know so much more about her and how she operated. Too bad that wasn't in the plan.

"Great class," he said when he really wanted to shower her with compliments.

"Thanks. You coming back tomorrow?"

Dirk stepped closer, even though he risked offending her if he did stink. He'd piled on the deodorant, but he'd also worked hard. "I was hoping to spend some more time with you today."

She arched her eyebrows, her teal blue eyes so appealing he could hardly stand not to touch her. "You can hope in one hand

and spit in the other, but it'll never get you the date with me. Why don't you just ask me out, Harvard grad?"

Dirk chuckled. She was cute. He wasn't sure why he'd told her about Harvard or admitted he'd been in the military. He kept personal details out of his undercover stories and usually didn't feel the need to inflate his own status.

"Sorry," he said, and he was. "I'm not interested in dating you. I'd like to hire you for personal training." He hated that he had to say it, but he needed to stop this, or he'd be begging her for a date and beyond. In control, that was him. Always. Except for last night when he'd lost his mind and kissed her outside the restaurant bathroom.

Her eyes lost their sparkle. She glanced over his chest and arms before meeting his gaze again. He didn't like how cold and tight her expression had suddenly become. "You don't look like you need my help." She turned and started instructing the class. "Welcome, friends. Start out with a lunge with a twist."

Dirk stood behind her, befuddled. Had she just turned down a training opportunity, or an opportunity to spend time with him? As her boss it annoyed him to think she'd turn down work. As the man who'd kissed her last night it was exasperating to think she'd turn down *him*. No woman turned him down. Yet he was probably confusing her as much as he was confusing himself. He'd just said he wasn't interested in dating her. Obviously, she didn't appreciate that line.

"Looks great, ladies. Now inchworms."

Dirk eased around to her side and said, "Did you just refuse to train me?"

Kit tilted her head up toward him and pursed her lips. "Has a woman ever refused you anything in your life?"

He blinked at her. She had no idea. His mom refused to love him. Melanie died.

"I didn't think so. Get used to rejection." She walked away from him and commanded, "Down into a plank." Then she started instructing individual women on form, completely ignoring him. The all-female class participants were taking turns gawking at him, a redhead winking obnoxiously at him when they turned into a side plank.

Dirk knew he should leave, but Kit was ticking him off now. Was she mad because he'd said he didn't want a date? Had the kiss last night *not* affected her, or had it affected her too much?

He did the last thing he should and trailed after her. She instructed the class to do pushups and was crouched down helping a lady perfect her form when he reached her. Glaring up at him, she said, "What do you want?"

"You," he said.

Her eyes widened, and he felt half the class suck in a breath.

"Not like that." He glared around at everybody. "I want a personal training appointment."

She stood and rolled her eyes. "Why? You're obviously perfect." She flung a hand at him. "And I specialize in training women."

"That's sexist."

"Oh, goodness, cry me a river."

Dirk smiled, despite the anger and confusion roiling in him. Even when he was in an undercover boss role, he could usually guide the situation. There was something about his confidence and knowledge that just inspired people to listen to what he had to say. Kit was throwing everything out of whack. "Do you have an opening to train me this afternoon?" he asked as nicely as possible.

Kit ignored him and barked, "To your stations. The workout is on the board."

An older lady stormed up to them and glared at him. "I don't like the bite in your voice today, Miss Kit. Do you need a hug?"

"Yes, Julie, I sure do." Kit opened her arms and Dirk felt jealous of a fifty-year old woman. When he'd kissed Kit, he'd only allowed their lips to touch, but somehow, she'd still yanked from him a tenderness he didn't know he possessed. When she touched his arm earlier, he wanted to pledge his devotion to one woman. And now, he wanted to be the one holding her close, memorizing the feel of her trim body against his.

Kit released Julie and smiled. "Everybody ready?"

"Yes!" They all cheered.

"Timer starts, now!"

The ladies started working and Kit hurried to instruct. Dirk trailed after her like a sap. The purchase of this gym may have been the worst idea he'd ever had. For once he should listen to his father, run to his L.A. office, and then hide in his Malibu mansion until his longing for her went away. Well not fully listen to his father. He could never "settle down".

Kit ignored him for several rounds of the workout, and then finally she whirled on him and snapped, "I have an opening at one."

He stepped back and inclined his chin, "I'll look forward to seeing you then."

Kit rolled her eyes and folded her arms across her chest. "You'll be the only one looking forward to it."

Dirk appreciated the sass behind her sharp response and recognized he probably deserved it for saying he wasn't interested in dating her. But how else could he protect himself? She was like a Siren luring men in. He wasn't some foolish sailor.

He turned and hurried away. He'd come back at one because he needed to evaluate his gym and her abilities. It was all professional from here on out. He wouldn't allow Kit Abbott to get under his skin any longer. Yet he was very afraid that he was going to sink faster than a sailor who'd tried to get to the lovely Siren and rammed his ship onto a reef.

CHAPTER FIVE

K it finished her morning classes at ten and was relieved to say goodbye to her last participant. That alone made her mad. Usually she had so much fun with her friends she hated to say goodbye. She started into her own workout and pushed herself hard for an hour before cleaning up all the stations.

Rushing home, she showered and ate a quick lunch before heading back to the gym for a noon training appointment. Dirk would be there at one. She seethed as she thought of him. Why had he flirted shamelessly with her, kissed her last night, showed up at her early morning workout class, and been so appealing and fun? Then when she gave him the slam dunk of an opening to ask her out, he slammed the door instead?

I'm not interested in dating you.

Those horrific words rolled around in her mind. If he wasn't interested why had he played her like that? Truthfully, she couldn't remember the last man who hadn't been interested in her. The only one that came to mind was Slade, but she was thrilled about that because he loved her best friend.

She finished her noon training appointment at five minutes to one, and who was waiting by the door? None other than the heartbreaker himself: Dirk Miller. What an absolute jerk. She'd known from the first time she saw him that he was the ultimate player, but his kiss last night had told her otherwise. Kit rolled her eyes at herself. She needed to put that kiss from her mind and focus on kicking his perfect backside through a workout. He'd be so sore and tired, he wouldn't have the energy to rile her up.

"Hey." He smiled a greeting as if nothing had transpired between them. He must've showered as he smelled clean and musky and looked unbelievably fit in a blue t-shirt and gray shorts.

Kit lifted a clipboard off the counter. "Please fill out the medical and training questionnaire and sign the liability waiver."

He nodded and reached for the clipboard. Their hands brushed as she passed it over, and she jolted from the warm connection that surged through her. He jerked as if he'd felt something as well. Oh, cripes, she couldn't freak out every time she touched him. She was hands-on with her clients. How could she avoid it training him for the next hour?

While he wrote she rushed around the open gym getting weights, boxes, and ropes ready. She adjusted resistance on the cable machines and thought through the next hour. She smelled his musky cologne as he came up close to her and extended the clipboard.

"Thanks," she murmured, being very careful not to touch him. "For your first training session we'll do a circuit, and then I'll study the information you gave me. Our next meeting will be more specific to your health, needs, and desires."

"My desires?" The deep, throaty way he said that made her stomach lift like she'd jumped off a cliff.

Kit bravely met his gaze. His eyes were impossibly blue, and they were drawing her in so fast she felt dizzy. She swallowed hard and managed to get out, "Desires for your fitness goals."

He lifted his chin. "Ah, I see."

He was doing it again. Flirting and making her want him. He didn't want a date so why was he confusing her like this? "Are you sure you want to do this?" she demanded, clinging to the clipboard.

His smile was like a slow burn, it grew and covered his face, making his eyes twinkle. "Do *what* exactly?"

Kit stepped back and pinned him with a glare. "What I meant was you already completed a demanding workout early this morning. Are you sure you want to suffer through an even harder workout right now or would you rather wait until tomorrow? No matter how tough you look, I have a feeling you'll be begging for mercy."

Dirk's smile stayed in place. Luckily, he didn't reach out and touch her, or she'd be the one begging him to date her. She basically had begged at this morning's class and he'd rejected her. "Ah, that's what you meant," he said.

She set the clipboard down on the counter and strode to the

ropes. "Let's get to work." Dirk obediently followed her every command, slamming the heavy ropes into the floor time and time again, maxing out the cable machine with hardly a grunt, working his way up to leaping onto and off a platform so high she worried he'd scrape his shin. He was obviously athletic and in shape. He was also very, very easy on the eyes. Watching him workout was ... tantalizing was the only word she could think of. She'd think he was killing himself to impress her ... if she didn't have the remembrance of him telling her this morning that he didn't want to date her. Why had he said that and ruined everything? Why did she even care? She had men lining up to date her and didn't need him.

The workout was almost done, and Dirk had sweat dripping down his face. She was proud of herself that she'd pushed him hard, but even prouder that she'd refrained from touching him. His form was exceptional so she hadn't needed to touch him to correct it, but she reached for him a few times before stopping herself. Was it simply her fingers yearning to feel him again? That was lame and weak, and she wasn't a weak woman.

She finished up with alternating sets of supermans for the lower back and plank holds for his abs. During the final minute of the plank, Kit could see she'd finally exhausted him. He let out a soft grunt of frustration as his lower back started rounding and his abs dipped slightly toward the floor. His form had been so perfect, she knew the only way he'd let himself slip, even this small amount, was if he was absolutely done.

Kit couldn't sit by. She bent low and wrapped her hands around the sides of his abdomen, tugging his body straight from head to toe. "Come on, Dirk, you've got this."

The muscles of his abdomen were rigid underneath her finger-tips and excitement rushed through her from this simple touch. She could feel how intensely he was straining to stay in the correct position. She'd trained many, many people but had never been more impressed with someone's grit, determination, and fitness level than she was today.

The timer went off and Kit released him. "You did it!" She pushed the button to silence the timer. Dirk rolled over, but accidentally knocked into her legs. She was still bent over and focused on the timer. Tripping onto him, she cried out in surprise. He cushioned her fall with his body and his arms auto-matically wrapped around her.

"What are you doing?" she squeaked, tremors of desire rushing through her.

He grinned. "That was actually an accident, but honestly? I have no clue."

"You're all sweaty," she said, but she made no move to free herself.

"Is that the only thing that's bothering you right now?" His eyebrow quirked up and his handsome face mocked her.

Kit pushed from his arms, and thankfully he let her go. As strong as he was, she wouldn't stand a chance if he wanted to restrain her. She jumped to her feet and backed up a step. Dirk stood slowly, and she was able to appreciate every glorious inch of him.

"I don't date clients," she threw at him.

"Good because I don't date anyone." The smile on his face was mocking, but there was something in his blue eyes that revealed he was as confused by the pull between them as she was.

"What are you talking about? You're the ultimate flirt. I'm sure you date a different girl every night."

He stepped closer, and the sheer manliness of him made her want to fling her arms around him again, explore those glorious muscles in his chest with her fingertips. *He's sweaty. He's a jerk. He doesn't want you.* None of her thoughts were helping. *Please, Lord, give me strength.*

"I go on dates," he murmured. "I don't date seriously."

Kit pushed out a breath. At least he was honest in his player status. "Good thing we understand each other."

"Good thing." His gaze slowly traveled over her, full of hunger and longing. Kit swallowed hard but couldn't swallow away how much she wanted to know this man better. She tried to remind herself she hated riddles, and Dirk Miller was definitely a riddle, but he was so appealing and intriguing it was hard to find any professionalism within herself.

"Was your workout satisfactory, sir?" she asked, a bit too breathlessly.

Dirk nodded. "I can see why you get such good reviews as a trainer."

"You've been Googling me?" she asked tartly, secretly loving that he had.

"You have no idea."

Kit flushed with pleasure but tried not to reveal it. "You're going to be sore. I hope for your sake you don't have to work at Sushi Sticks tonight."

"I've been working since four a.m.," he said, but then he kind of jolted like he shouldn't have said that.

"You have a second job?" she asked. Four a.m.? Did struggling artists or writers wake up at four a.m.? Who knew what he was, or what he did? He took vague and mysterious to a new level.

"You could say that." His infuriating smirk was back. "I run a side business."

"Oh?" She hoped he'd tell her about it but wished she didn't care. Unfortunately, she didn't have another training appointment today, so she didn't have a reason to make him leave.

He didn't explain. "How much do I owe you?" he asked.

"How much do you make per hour?" she asked.

"Excuse me?" His brow squiggled.

"I charge my clients what they make per hour."

He reared back like she was insane. "So if somebody is making ten dollars an hour you only make ten dollars training them?"

She nodded.

"That's an insult to your expertise."

"Thank you, but it's how I charge."

"What if they work on commission, like a car salesman, or on tips, like a waiter?"

She shrugged. "I trust that they'll average what they make per hour and be fair with me."

"What if they are a lawyer who bills out at a thousand dollars an hour?"

"Lucky me."

He simply stared at her then shook his head and said, "That's insane."

Kit smiled, liking that she'd ruffled him. "It works well for me and all my clients seem to think it's fair."

"What does management think?"

"I'm the management," she threw at him.

His eyebrows lifted. "Oh? Do you own the gym also?"

"No." If only she did, so she didn't have to bow to that jerk Colin Johanson.

"What does the owner think?"

Kit didn't like the reference to the guy who had just bought the gym. What would he think? She doubted that he would like it. "The previous owner didn't care, the gym takes twenty percent, and the way I charge averages out to be around a hundred dollars an hour, close to the high end of the going rate for training in the city. Sausalito's a well-to-do area and my clients like me."

"The previous owner? What does the *current* owner think?"

"I don't know, and I don't care."

Dirk flinched but didn't say anything. She really should be doing some research this afternoon and finding a way to start her own gym, so she didn't have to deal with the new owner at all. Could she use her home as collateral? What if she had to ask one of her brothers or her parents to co-sign? That would be rough on her. They all adored her, sometimes too much, but as the youngest in the family she had to stand on her own. "Look, I need to get going."

Dirk held up a finger. "Let me get you some cash."

Kit felt awkward, most of her clients were set up on automatic withdrawal or they paid her through Venmo. Cash felt ... off, personal for some strange reason. Cash wasn't personal, but Dirk definitely was. He was getting deep under her skin, and she didn't like it.

Dirk sauntered to the side of the entryway where there was a wall of cubby holes for people to put keys, jackets, etc. He grabbed a phone, keys, and a wallet from a cubby. Walking back to her, he flipped open the wallet and pulled out five hundred-dollar bills. Kit's eyes widened as she saw there were a lot more large bills left in his leather wallet.

"You left that fat wad of cash in a cubby hole at a gym?"

Dirk shrugged. "It's only you and me here. I figured if you stole it, you needed it more than I do."

"You're crazy."

"I've heard that one before." He put the bills in her hand then gently closed her fingers over them. Fire traced through her from his touch. Why did this guy, who had bluntly told her he wasn't interesting in dating her, and also seemed to have a lot he was hiding, affect her so much? Why couldn't she have felt like this when Mike gave her a hug goodnight last night?

"You make five hundred dollars per hour?" she asked, pulling her hand back and clinging to the money.

"On occasion." The way he smiled at her was like she was a clueless teenage girl. "Thanks for a killer workout. I'd say I'll be back tomorrow, but I might not be able to walk after double torture from you today."

"You might need an Epsom salt bath."

Dirk chuckled. "Real men don't take baths."

"Do they take showers?"

"Yes. Especially if they know a beautiful lady will be joining them for dinner that night."

"You don't date," she reminded him, ignoring the thrill that went through her.

"I might make an exception for you."

His gaze traveled over her, and Kit's heart walloped against her chest. The fact that he'd admitted he was a player and had her more confused and stirred up than she ever remembered being, paled in comparison to the ache to take him up on his offer.

"I already have dinner plans," she said breathily.

"My loss." He gave her one more smile then turned and strutted from the gym. Pushing out the glass doors, he didn't even look back before climbing into an Audi sport utility. She could see a rental sticker in the window. What kind of a waiter had an eighty-thousand dollar vehicle for a rental car? She'd assumed he lived here. Why have a rental car at all? Maybe his regular car was in the shop, and he hit the lottery of car rentals?

Kit weakly shuffled to the gym counter and leaned heavily against it. She uncrumpled the cash in her hand and stared at it. Five hundred dollars? He "occasionally" made that per hour? Who was Dirk Miller, and how was she going to get him out of her head?

CHAPTER SIX

Dirk went to Sushi Sticks that night, because he needed a break from the mountain of work on his laptop, he loved their food, and he liked being around his employees at the intimate restaurant. He always had more work than hours in the day, another reason he assumed his dad got so frustrated that he wasted time "playing undercover boss and not settling down".

He ate a California roll with lobster on top and a roll with raw salmon, tuna, avocado, cream cheese, and cilantro while he chatted with the cooks.

"Hey, boss," Natalie glided into the kitchen and grinned at him.

"Hi, Natalie."

"You know the gorgeous blonde you were flirting with by the bathroom last night?"

Dirk's smile froze, but his heartbeat increased. He didn't know

Natalie had seen them, but the more pressing issue was anything she had to tell him about Kit. He couldn't seem to help himself from flirting with her. It bugged him to feel out of control, but it was also exhilarating and addicting. He couldn't think of a woman who had affected him like this, not since he'd been a hormone-driven teenager.

"Yes?" he said, trying to appear casual though he leaned forward, and he knew his eyes probably betrayed him.

Natalie smirked. "She's here again. Having dinner with a couple of good-looking blond dudes."

Dirk pushed out a heavy breath. Apparently one date wasn't enough for the tempting Kit Abbott. "Hmm," he said noncommittally.

"You want to wait on them?"

"Not really." He wouldn't mind flirting with Kit again, but seeing her with two men didn't appeal to him. Jealousy wasn't a companion he beckoned to, and he'd felt it strongly last night as Kit ate, talked, and laughed with the football superstar, Mike Kohler. "I'm not dressed to serve anyway."

"If she excuses herself to the restroom, I'll let you know."

Dirk chuckled. "Thanks. You do that."

Natalie grabbed the plates ready to serve and sashayed back out of the kitchen. The cooks, dishwashers, and one of the waiters were all staring at him.

"So, have you all been to a Giants' game at Oracle Park?" Dirk asked.

A couple of them nodded.

"I got a suite for a week from next Monday's game. I thought with the restaurant closed on Mondays, you all could come ... if you want."

Several of them were nodding vigorously, their eyes wide. "We'd love to, sir," Johnny, the head waiter, said.

"Great. You can each bring a couple guests as well. The suite holds forty, and they'll provide dinner, drinks, and snacks."

Dirk hid a grin at the excitement shining in their faces. This was one of the things he loved to do for employees—provide experiences they typically didn't get. He refused to dwell on the fact that he also did over-the-top activities like this because he was lonely and had nobody to hang out with. He had college friends, military friends, and work friends but he traveled too much to see any of them often.

The swinging door to the kitchen burst open. "She went to the bathroom," Natalie rushed to say.

Dirk's heartbeat raced, but he didn't move. "Thanks for letting me know."

Natalie planted her hands on her hips. "Hurry, go! Who knows how long she'll be in there."

Dirk thought sometimes it was detrimental that he worked amongst his employees as a peer before he revealed who he was. But Natalie was staring at him so expectantly, and his palms were sweating, and he really, really wanted to tease Kit and see her reaction. He just had to make sure he stayed in control and didn't touch her or kiss her. His reaction to her when he'd accidentally knocked her on top of him at the gym, and then impulsively held her there was caveman primitive. He wasn't that guy, ever. Okay, he'd been that guy twice with Kit, kissing her outside the bathroom last night when she was on a date, and then holding her against his chest today.

Be in control, he repeated in his head as he ignored his employees' whispers and sauntered out into the restaurant. He scanned the busy dining room and saw two blond guys sitting in the middle of the room with a place setting that was empty. They looked like successful guys who nobody pushed around. In another reality, he'd probably think they could be friends of his. Just not in his obsessed-with-Kit reality. They were the competition, and he didn't like them.

Stop it, he told himself. He rushed over to the sheltered alcove and waited outside the women's restroom. He wasn't sure what he was doing or how he'd react when Kit walked out. Feeling completely opposite of the successful, accomplished, and in-control businessman, he realized he really liked this rush, but even more terrifying—he really liked her.

K it washed her hands and dried them. She appreciated her brothers taking her out tonight while their wives hosted a baby shower for a family member. It was pretty cute that her sisters-in-law were cousins and best friends, and that her brothers both lived just down the street from her parents, driving into the city for work each day. Isaac was an accountant and Jake a lawyer. They both did well and were great to have around. She only wished Isaac had brought his baby girl Isabelle with him. When Jake said they were coming to Sushi Sticks she complained she'd been here last night. He begged, reminding her that his wife wouldn't eat sushi.

"Everybody has to have one fault," she'd told him and agreed to his restaurant choice. She loved the food and didn't mind helping her brother out. Once you were addicted to sushi, it was hard to get enough. She did mind the worry over running into Dirk again. Kit wasn't sure if she wanted to see him or not. He didn't appear to be working, and she'd finally settled down and stopped watching the kitchen entry for him.

Exiting the bathroom, she remembered the rush, better than jumping off a cliff, she'd experienced as she walked out last night and saw ... "Dirk!"

He leaned casually against the opposite wall. He was wearing a short-sleeved, blue Henley and gray Volcom shorts. The blue brought out the blue in his eyes, and the short sleeves and shorts showed off his incredible build. She could still feel his abs under her fingertips as she'd helped him with the plank this morning. A flush of warmth and excitement started inside, and she hoped it didn't show on her face.

"Fancy meeting you here," he said. "I'm not sure if you're obsessed with sushi or just hoping to meet your favorite waiter in a secluded alcove." He grinned and slowly crossed the space toward her.

Kit stood her ground. She was not letting him back her into that wall and kiss her again. Kiss her again. Her lips seemed to tingle at the memory. "Obsessed with sushi," she managed to get out.

He nodded, stopping half a foot away. His delicious musky

cologne wrapped around her. She loved it, but she'd love his arms around her more. They'd only had brief touches and an even briefer kiss. If she snaked her arms around his waist and leaned her head into his chest would he simply hold her, or would he take possession of her mouth like the confident, in-control guy he was? Would the sparks from their bodies being aligned completely overwhelm her or make her feel like the world was in her hands? She forced herself to stop these fantasies in her mind.

"So." Dirk grinned at her, but his blue eyes looked suspiciously full of jealousy. "A date with the superstar, Mike Kohler, last night wasn't enough, you had to bring two guys tonight?"

Kit pressed her lips together to stop the laugh bubbling out. He thought she was on a date with her brothers? Gross, but funny. "Yeah." She lifted her shoulders. "It takes two men to tango with me."

"They must be the wrong guys then." He moved closer. "I could tango with you all by myself."

She arched her eyebrows. The thought of tangoing with him made her body flood with longing. "I don't know about that. I'd hate to damage your 'no-dating rule'."

"That is kind of rough. But if my memory of last night serves correct, I don't need to be on a date with you to get a sample of those lovely lips." He leaned in closer.

Kit almost melted into him. He was so appealing and confident. She loved a confident man, and at the moment she wanted to kiss him more than she wanted her own gym. But that was a jerky-thing for him to say. She pushed at his chest. "You don't get a sample if you don't pay the price."

Dirk chuckled and wrapped both his hands around hers, holding them against his chest. Kit's breathing stuttered, and her heart raced, but the world seemed to settle. Something in his touch and gaze said, *This is the man for you, Kit Abbott.* She blinked to clear the fog.

"What's the price?" he murmured, his eyes dropping to her lips then slowly, languidly making their way back to meet hers. She loved his bright blue eyes.

"More than you can afford," she snapped at him.

He grinned. "You know very little about me, Kit Abbott."

She swallowed hard. "And who's fault is that?" she asked.

He lifted his shoulders innocently. "Do you want to know more?" his voice was low, husky, and awe-inspiring, but also somehow vulnerable.

"Maybe," she admitted, cursing herself for being so weak. What this man did to her was not fair.

"Excuse me," a woman said from behind Dirk.

"Excuse us." Dirk kept hold of her hands and tugged Kit away from the door.

The woman smiled and went inside the restroom. Kit pulled her hands free. "I need to go."

He stared at her, something raw and painful in his blue eyes. "I don't like you on dates with other men."

"Oh, yeah? What are you going to do about it?"

"How late do you work tomorrow?"

"Classes are over at ten. I don't have any training appointments." Why was she telling him that? She should be telling him where to go. He only wanted to go on one date with her, and then discard her. Already she could sense it would shatter her somehow vulnerable-to-him heart. What was happening to her? Her heart had never really opened to anyone except her family and Mae.

He nodded. "I'll pick you up at the gym at ten-thirty. The late morning, afternoon, and evening are mine."

Kit knew she should want to rear up at him like a heckled cat for trying to claim her time, but she loved, loved a man who would take charge and be the man. She walked around him, but turned to look over her shoulder.

He was staring at her as if she were an angel. "Kit?" his voice was appealing and almost begging. No. Dirk was too confident to ever beg, but there was a pleading note there.

Kit caved much too quickly. "What should I wear?"

His face crinkled in an irresistible grin. "Bike shorts."

"Ooh, I look cute in those," she teased. Nobody looked cute in bike shorts.

"You'd look beautiful in anything."

Kit couldn't take it anymore. Either she ran back to her brothers or she knocked Dirk into the wall and took advantage of his mouth. "If you're lucky I'll be there," she managed to get out, the quaver in her voice betraying her. Turning, she hurried away.

"See you at ten-thirty," Dirk's voice came from behind her.

Kit didn't allow herself to look back, but she grinned as she walked back to her table. Tomorrow couldn't come soon enough. If only she wasn't so tied up in confused pretzels wondering what Dirk's intentions were and how he had gotten into her heart so easily.

CHAPTER SEVEN

Kit watched the door between each morning workout class, but Dirk didn't appear. She finished at ten a.m., foregoing her own workout, but still didn't have time to run home and shower. She used the gym's small shower, rinsing off quickly before dressing in bike shorts and a tank-top style bike jersey, putting on her clip-on bike shoes, smoothing her long hair into a clean ponytail, and putting on minimal makeup. She was waiting outside at ten-thirty when Dirk pulled up.

He had two Trek Emonda bikes on the rack of his rented sport utility. Popping out, he stared at her and then whistled, "You do make bike shorts look good." He looked really good in some baggy bike shorts, the expensive ones that had two layers so they didn't show off everything, and a fitted t-shirt.

Kit rolled her eyes and laughed. "Of course I do." She wrinkled her nose. "I have my own bike." It was in the gym and she had planned on riding it.

"As nice as these?" He put a hand on one of the bikes. She knew they were over fifteen grand each.

"No," she admitted. "How did you afford those?" Her eyes widened as she realized what she'd said.

Dirk didn't appear offended at all. "I told you I have a side business, and they're just rentals."

Kit wasn't aware of a bike shop willing to rent out a Trek Emonda. Many shops didn't even carry bikes that expensive. She only knew what they were because her brother Jake was big into road bike racing.

Dirk lifted one of the bikes off. "I told the owner your size and height. Hopefully he got the adjustments right."

"You think you know what I weigh?" Kit marched up to him, not sure if she was pleased or offended.

He looked her over. "I said one-thirty because you're about five-eight and you're thin, but you're also perfectly fit and muscle weighs more than people think."

She was closer to one-thirty-five. "Hmm. You're close."

He grinned. "Let's get you on the bike." He held the bike, and she strapped on her helmet, put a water bottle in the holder, and stowed her phone and keys in a little compartment behind the seat. Then she straddled the bike and clipped in her right foot. Pushing off, she clipped in her other shoe, and then pedaled around the almost-empty parking lot. "How is it?" he asked when she got closer.

"Almost as perfect as me," she teased. This ride felt like slicing through butter. Rented. Crazy. What if one of them wrecked?

Dirk laughed. "Good thing you threw the 'almost' in there."

Kit pedaled past, wanting to stop and savor the way he looked at her, but she was a mess over this guy, and she needed to calm down about how he made her feel. She had every indication that he was a player and heartbreaker.

He locked his car, put his water bottle in the holder, slung a backpack on, and pedaled up to her. "Which way?"

She headed north out of the parking lot but said, "Wait a second. Mr. In Charge hasn't planned exactly where he wants to go?"

"I'd like to go through Mill Valley and see Cascade Falls, but you're the local."

"That's a fun ride. Let's do it." They pedaled single file along side streets, then when they reached the asphalt bike path that led from Sausalito to Mill Valley, they went side-by-side and Kit said, "It's only about fourteen miles roundtrip and a short hike. Not much of a challenge for a tough guy like you." Not much of a workout for her either.

Dirk smiled. Even in bike shorts with a helmet on, he was irresistible. "My entire body aches from yesterday's workouts. I'm hoping the bike ride will loosen up my legs."

"Amazing."

"What's that?" He glanced at her.

"The humility it must've taken for you to admit that."

Smiling, he said, "Yeah, you'd better enjoy it, because you'll never see humility out of me again."

"I believe you."

He chuckled.

"I thought you were from around here, but you drive an expensive rental, rent fifteen-thousand dollar bikes, and have never been to Cascade Falls." When she glanced at him, his face was tight, and he was concentrating on the path flowing underneath them. "What gives? You're not really a waiter, are you?"

He did look at her then. "Of course I am."

Was he lying to her? "Where are you from?"

"L.A. originally, but I've become a wanderer lately."

"Does your other business make it possible for you to 'wander' in an Audi, renting top of the line bikes, and spending five hundred dollars on one personal training session?"

He smiled but it didn't reach his blue eyes. "I love these houseboats," he redirected the conversation.

"Floating homes," she corrected automatically.

"Oh, excuse me, floating homes. It'd be cool to live in one."

She flushed with pleasure. "I do."

"What?" He pressed on the brakes and cut to a stop.

Kit stopped also and glanced back at him.

"Which one?"

"You can't see mine from here, it's further south in the bay."

"Oh." He started pedaling and she did as well. "I bet it's incredible."

"It is. My grandparents gave it to me."

He asked questions about her house, her grandparents and the rest of her family, and then got into questions about her schooling and career. Kit enjoyed talking to him and the pleasant ride in the summer sun, but realized as they cruised through Mill Valley and up Cascade Drive toward the falls that he was an expert at focusing the conversation on her. He'd shared hardly anything about himself.

They reached the trailhead for the falls and stowed their bikes and helmets off the road a little bit, but Kit didn't like leaving them. "Anybody who knows anything about bikes will steal these."

"Aw, c'mon, where's your faith in humankind?"

"I have faith in the good Lord but not as much in all of his children."

Dirk stared at her. "You surprise me."

"Because I'm a believer?"

"No, that's evident by the light in your eyes. But good Christians love everyone else as much as they love their Savior, correct?"

Kit planted her hands on her hips, not appreciating the challenge. "I try to love people, but I don't just leave candy in front of a toddler and expect him to not eat it."

Dirk chuckled and wrapped his hand around hers. Warmth and joy threaded through her body as surely as his fingers threaded with hers. His laughter evaporated as he stared down at her hand then back up at her face; longing and surprise filled his blue eyes. Kit knew he had to feel what she felt when he touched her. She met his gaze and willed him to say something about it. She'd dated, held hands with, and kissed different men, and she knew he'd done the same with other women, but she'd never felt like this from a simple touch. They both knew there was something special between them. She refused to be the first one to say it. All her mental reminders that he was a player didn't make much difference to her at the moment. She wanted Dirk Miller.

He tugged at her hand. "Let's go check out the waterfall."

"But the bikes," she insisted, not falling into step with him.

"Are insured." His easy smile returned, but he didn't let go of her hand as they walked slowly up the packed dirt path. It wasn't as comfortable walking in their bike shoes as running or hiking shoes would've been, but it wasn't a very long hike. They walked through thick greenery, pine and redwood trees towering above them shading the path, a creek bed down below the left-hand side of the trail. This time of year the creek was only trickling, and the waterfall wouldn't be spectacular, but it was quiet, cool, and peaceful, and she liked being alone with Dirk. She really liked holding his hand.

"You don't act like a waiter," she said.

Dirk chuckled. "I've only been a waiter for a couple of weeks. I flit from job to job."

"Yet you can afford to rent an Audi and Trek Emondas flitting from job to job?"

He shrugged his shoulders. "My side business does well."

"What is it?"

His mouth pursed. "Property management. This is a great shady hike. The bike ride was great too, just a little warm."

She let him skirt more questions, for now. The questions with this guy were just piling up, and she wasn't sure what to think about him or any of the information he'd given her. What was he hiding and why? They reached the waterfall. As she'd imagined, it was more of a trickle, but it was still pretty with the greenery surrounding them in the quiet spot.

Sneaking a glance at him, she caught him looking at her instead of the view. "What do you think of the scenery?" she asked.

"Beautiful." He gave her that irresistible smirk she was becoming far too attached to, and then looked around. "The waterfall is beautiful too."

Kit pushed at him with her shoulder. "Don't worry. I won't let your empty flattery go to my head."

"Empty flattery? That hurts. I think you are the most beautiful woman I've ever met." He squeezed her hand, and the tone of his voice was not joking.

Kit mumbled, "Thank you." She wasn't sure what else to say. Many men had raved about her beauty, but the sincerity in Dirk's deep voice was unmatched. "I like your voice," she said.

"My voice?" Dirk laughed. "I tell you you're the most beautiful woman in the world and you admit that you like my voice?"

Kit laughed as well. "Unlike some people, I don't hand out compliments like lollipops." She focused on him instead of the scenery. "You already know that you're perfect looking."

"Oh, I do?" His grin made his face even more appealing to her. "So tell me, how am I supposed to 'know that I'm perfect looking'?"

"Come on." She rolled her eyes. "You've dated every girl and her sister, and they've all fallen under your charming spell."

"So, you think I'm charming and perfect looking?" He winked.

She laughed and didn't give him the satisfaction of an answer.

"But why do you think I'm some *Romeo*?" He drawled it out in a lilting voice. "I told you I don't date, and I definitely don't wear tights." He gestured to his bike shorts that were more of a cargo style with the awkward butt pad hidden underneath.

"You avoided the tights nicely," she admitted. "But you said you 'go on dates you just don't date'."

"Have you memorized everything I've said?"

"Pretty much." She released his hand and faced him. "Especially when you told me, and I quote, 'I'm not interested in dating you'."

Dirk winced. "I'm sorry. That ..."

"Didn't come out right?" she supplied, hoping he would retract the statement and lay out there his interest in developing a relationship.

"No, actually it did."

Kit's jaw dropped, and she backed away. Dirk didn't come after her. He pushed a hand through his hair and shook his head. "Look. You're amazing—beautiful, talented, funny, smart, pure, lit up from the inside. If I was looking for a woman to date seriously, I'd be chasing you so hard you wouldn't stand a chance."

"I'd reject you so fast your head would spin," she hurtled back at him.

Dirk gave her a sad smile. "You're the only woman who could reject me."

"Oh, cocky, Zeus-like man. It's getting sticky in this forest." She had to try to act feisty while inside she was falling apart. She'd been falling for him fast and hard, and now he was rejecting her?

"Because no other woman has a chance to get to me," he said, tilting his head and studying her.

Her chest felt tight, and her own head was spinning. Dirk was either a master at head games or he was damaged from something in his past. Either way he was going to hurt her like he had when he'd told her he didn't want to date her. Nobody had hurt her before. "Why'd you con me into this date and hold my hand and tell me how beautiful I am just to make me feel like crap again?"

"Because I'm weak," he said without hesitation.

She guffawed. "That's ridiculous. You're a jerk, but you're definitely not weak."

"I am." His voice got more intense. "I'm weak like my father. Why else would I allow myself to fall for you?" His face froze. He blinked, and now he was the one backing up a few steps.

"Dirk?" She tentatively crossed toward him.

"Please, don't." He shook his head, and then folded his arms across his chest.

She was the one freezing now. What was happening? Dirk was flirtatious one moment, withdrawn the next. She didn't know what to think around him or how to react. He'd fallen for her? That line had made her want to cheer, but the way he'd reacted to his own words made her cold inside. He thought his father was weak and at that moment he'd realized he shared a characteristic with him. She wished she knew what it meant, how to help. She didn't think there was anything weak about Dirk and everyone had faults, things they didn't like about themselves.

He finally unclenched his arms and stepped back toward her. "I swear you're like a Siren who lures men in. That's what all these feelings are, right? The warmth, the connection, the desire to stay with you until I'm old and bald."

Kit's heart was going so fast she was trembling. She hardly knew him, yet she felt the same and to hear him admit it gave her a hope she didn't know if she dared trust. "You feel all those things around me?"

"Yes!" He flung at her. "Why? Why are you doing this to me? How?"

"Oh, Dirk, I'm not trying to do anything to you. These feelings are as foreign to me as they seem to be to you."

He simply stared at her, as if trying to distinguish if she were telling the truth and obviously, trying to hold himself distant from her.

She made a rash and possibly idiotic decision as she closed the distance between them and wrapped her arms around his lower back.

Dirk startled, and he didn't hug her back, but he didn't push her away either. Kit should've been as terrified as he seemed to be, this was uncharted territory for her and no amount of dates with different men could've prepared her for how Dirk made her feel. Quite the opposite—she assumed no man could affect her and had almost given up on looking for the man of her dreams. How wrong she'd been.

With a mix of power and light surging through her body, she pressed in close to him and laid her head in the crook of his neck. Even though it was invigorating, there was also a settled feeling deep inside that told her this was her spot. She'd hoped someday she'd find this spot, this rightness with one man but had assumed that day was far in the future, or would never come. She said a prayer of gratitude to the good Lord for leading Dirk to her.

Kit loved his musky scent and the sensation of his strong body against hers, as she ran her hands up his muscular back and wrapped her arms and hands the length of his upper back. His body was coiled as if they were in an action movie, and the bad guys were going to leap from behind the wide redwood tree trunks. Was that something to do with his military training or how afraid he was to give himself to her? He still didn't hug her back, but he pressed in against her, and that gave her hope.

Kit tilted her head up to look into his face. He was staring at her, his blue eyes filled with tenderness, desire, and wariness.

"Hold me," she whispered.

Dirk was much too serious as he stared at her. "I can't be my father," he murmured.

She had no clue what that meant, but she said decisively, "You aren't."

Dirk's eyes searched hers. She wasn't sure what he was looking for, what he was thinking. Kit had never been the sappy fool who threw herself at a man. Is that what she was doing right now? Yet the rightness of being close to Dirk radiated through her. This was where she was meant to be. She had to try one more time, "Hold me, Dirk."

Dirk hesitated before his arms came around her back, and he cradled her in close. The breath rushed from Kit's lungs. If she'd thought holding him was powerful, him returning it was like an inferno. Hope and desire raged through her. He simply held her for a few beautiful moments, and then he trailed his hands up her back and along her neck, making her tremble. His hands came around and cupped her cheeks. He tilted her head slightly up, so she was inches from his lips.

He let out a soft groan and murmured, "Ah, Kit."

She smiled tremulously up at him, willing herself not to cry. The tears pricking at the corners of her eyelids were not sad tears but emotional, overcome tears. She was not the overly-emotional person, ever, but this beautiful moment with Dirk was so unexpected and powerful, she felt dazed by it.

His gaze widened when one stubborn tear spilled over and raced down her cheek. "Kit?" his obvious concern for her made more tears spring up, each fighting to spill over.

"I'm okay," she insisted. "I'm not sad."

"Then why are you crying?" He didn't release her face from his hands, but she felt him withdrawing.

Kit clung tighter to his upper back. "I've never felt a connection like this. It's overpowering and beautiful."

He nodded. "I know," he said quietly.

"I'm not the weepy type, and I don't want to be crying about this power surging between us."

"What should we do about it?" he asked, staring at her, as if she had all the answers.

"Kiss until we know what direction to go." It was a bold thing to say.

Dirk smiled, but his eyes were still sober. "I don't know if that's the solution. I've watched one too many Marvel movies. What if one of us explodes from the power surge?"

Kit laughed uneasily. "I'm willing to take the risk ... are you?"

She met his gaze head on and held tight to his muscular back. His well-built body overshadowed hers, and she wanted to draw from his strength and give strength back to him. She wanted him. That realization was terrifying and exhilarating. Maybe more terrifying at the moment, as she didn't know him very well and had no clue if he returned her feelings. He'd acknowledged the connection, but he was definitely holding back.

Dirk's blue eyes were smiling at her, but there was something deep in his gaze. He was as scared as she was and just as unfamiliar with the treacherous waters they were navigating. She was surging down white-water rapids with no paddle or guide, praying there wasn't a leak in the raft.

"Come on," she taunted softly. "I double-dog dare you."

"Whew." Dirk pursed his mouth and blew out a breath. "The double-dog dare. You had to go straight there?"

Kit smiled. She liked how they could tease, but every nerve seemed to be tingling and on red-alert. She needed his kiss, and she needed it now, but he'd shown every indication that he was a man and was also dealing with some issues from his father, apparently. She wasn't going to force her lips on his. He needed to step up right now and kiss her.

"At the moment I'd go about anywhere for you," she murmured. The words were out before she could call them back. She'd made herself vulnerable for him, she'd begged him, Kit was as uncomfortable and unfamiliar with all of this as he was. It was his move now, and she'd never had so much invested in a man's decision, because she'd never let a man into her heart before.

"Kit." He said her name so tenderly in a deep, husky voice that made her tremble. His eyes trailed over her face one more time, as soft as a caress, then he bent his head and made her his.

The warm pressure of his mouth covering hers sent an explosion of desire through her, but stronger than that was the rightness of their becoming one. She clung to him as he tilted her head with his hands and explored her mouth with his. Dirk Miller was the man for her, and she knew that as surely as she knew that the Savior, her family, and Mae loved her. No one but Dirk would ever do for her.

Their lips continued the intricate dance, and it was beautiful, almost sacred to her in this quiet spot, their sanctuary from the world, from anyone else mattering to them at all. Dirk was all that mattered to her, and she was going to make him hers as surely as his lips had branded her his.

He pulled back abruptly, his breath coming hard and fast. Their foreheads touched as he continued to cradle her face. His blue eyes were full of her, but then they filled with concern and fear. He released her and stepped quickly back.

Kit was dizzy from his kiss and even more so from him stepping away. "Dirk," it came out as a needy whimper. Kit hated that. She wasn't the needy woman. Men pursued her, but this was Dirk and even with as little as she knew about him, she wasn't above acknowledging that she'd do anything for him.

She stepped toward him, but he held up a hand, as if warding her off. "Please, Kit. Don't."

"Don't what?"

"Don't touch me again."

Kit's heart dropped painfully. He was retreating. She shook herself mentally, and refused to pursue him. If he returned her feelings, she'd go to the ends of the earth for him. On the other hand, if he didn't want her it would rip her apart, but she would never let him know that.

"I can't, Kit, you don't understand. This isn't you, it's me."

"So, the classic, 'It's not you, it's me'?" She folded her arms across her chest but couldn't protect herself, not when she'd already given him everything, and now he was telling her he couldn't. He couldn't, what? "What don't I understand? Why can't you ... whatever you can't do?"

He shook his head, refusing to answer her. Long, painful seconds trickled by slower than the stream was moving. Kit wanted to grab him and kiss him until he knew exactly why they needed to be together. Yet ... he hadn't felt what she'd felt, or he wouldn't be rejecting her like this.

She backed away, and he didn't reach for her or say anything, he simply watched her with a tortured expression. Anger and embarrassment finally overtook her stupid, smitten heart. "Well, don't worry about it then," she snapped. "It's no skin off my butt if you don't want something to develop between us." She forced out an unsteady bark of a laugh. "I've got men crawling to my door, begging me to date them, I don't need you." Such lame lies on her part. Yes, men were after her nonstop, but Dirk was the only one she needed. Yet, if he didn't need or want her, she'd have to put up a shield and act tough. She had some pride and confidence left and wasn't about to be the one to grovel.

Dirk simply stared at her. He didn't have the graciousness to beg for her to love him, or at the very least appear jealous that another man could take his place. Sadly, she didn't know that anyone could ever take his place, not after what she'd just felt in his arms.

He finally forced a smile and muttered, "Well that's good." He laughed, and it sounded awkward and weird in the quiet forest. "Of course you have men begging for even a minute of your time. Look at the past two nights, different dates with different men." He nodded, though his eyes looked tortured. "That's great. I'm glad it's worked out, and we both understand each other. This was all just a fun ... fling."

Kit was the one staring now. Either the sparks between them were all one-sided, or he was completely deluding himself to make this less painful. Less painful for him at least. It was obvious he wasn't going to admit to what he felt. If he even felt anything. She had never been so mortified. No boy or man had ever rejected her, and now the one she had imagined for a brief second was her destiny was openly rejecting her. It was written all over his face.

She couldn't even fake a response that would show how unaffected she was by him. Whirling away from him, she took off at a hard run down the trail. Every foot strike was loud and painful in her biking shoes. She was probably ruining the clips and giving herself an injury, but she didn't care. All she wanted was to get far away from Dirk Miller and never have to see that look of him rejecting her on his face. She hated that he obviously felt badly about it. Well, he didn't need to feel sorry for her because she was fine.

His footsteps pounded behind hers, both of them sounding unnatural and out of place in the quiet forest. She'd felt like this spot was their sanctuary, and now they'd ruined it, rejected the gift given them from above of the most pure and beautiful kiss and connection she'd ever experienced.

"Kit!" Dirk called out, a pleading, desperate note in his voice.

Kit ignored him and finally reached the trailhead and their bikes. She grabbed the one she'd been riding and lifted it over to the road. It was light, and she moved fast, but Dirk still caught her.

"Kit. Please." He was breathing heavily. He put his hands up and requested, "Please don't."

"Don't what?" she demanded, clinging to the bike and wishing with everything in her that Dirk would touch her arm or her hand, but he kept his distance.

"I don't like seeing you ... upset."

Kit harrumphed at him. That was his idea of an apology? "I don't really care what you like," she said. Throwing her leg over the bike, she clipped in her right foot. Dirk reached out to her, but then his hands stopped midair. Now he was afraid to even touch her? She growled in frustration and pushed off. Dirk was close enough he could've stopped her, but he didn't. She saw him rushing for his bike.

Kit coasted down Cascade Drive. She had to stop and fumble to strap on her helmet, but then she pushed off again and pedaled furiously. With her leg speed and the decline, she was flying. She'd never ridden this fast. It was unnerving and might've been a rush, if she wasn't so mad at Dirk. He caught up with her before the end of Cascade Drive and trailed her through the town of Mill Creek, and then onto the bike trail past the bay and her neighborhood of floating houses. Neither of them said anything as they pumped through the miles. Kit was grateful it was only seven miles, as even being this close to Dirk was painful and made her want to jump off her bike, knock him off his, kiss him again, and then be the one to choose to walk away. If she physically could walk away with how much she yearned for him.

Tears spilled out and flew away in the wind. It was only because they were going so fast, and the wind was stinging her eyes because she didn't have sunglasses on. It had nothing to do with the heartbreaking jerk behind her.

Finally, finally they made it to Sausalito, and then pulled into her parking lot. Well, maybe not her parking lot much longer. She'd done nothing to comply with the new owner's wishes or find her own space and secure a loan for her new gym. More unwanted tears appeared. She blinked them away. Frustration over work, that's what this was. She needed her friend, Mae, right now.

Braking, she hurried to leap off the bike. She wanted to set it on the ground or prop it against Dirk's vehicle, but she couldn't do it. The bike and the vehicle were worth too much to scratch. She propped it against her side as she pulled her keys and her phone out of the pouch on the bike.

Dirk stopped next to her, got off his bike, and quickly lifted and secured it on the rack. He turned and took her bike. "Thanks," he murmured. Pivoting, he lifted it onto the rack.

Kit tugged her helmet off, set her keys and phone in the upside down helmet, and backed away, clinging to the helmet's strap. She didn't know if she should go hide in her gym, jump in her car and race away, or follow her body's instincts to knock Dirk down and kiss him again. She yearned to simply touch him, and a small part of her believed if they kissed again he'd have to acknowledge the bonds already formed between them. It was a very small part though and not worth risking the last shards of her pride.

He turned to her before she could work a solution or exit strategy out in her mind. Offering a pained smile, he said, "I'm sorry, Kit."

That ticked her off. She dropped her helmet on the ground, stormed toward him, and jabbed a finger into his chest. "No. You don't get the right to say sorry and think that's going to fix this." He'd broken her heart, which was crazy as she hadn't even consciously given it to him to break, and no one had ever had the privilege of getting that close before. She vowed no one ever would again. Especially not Dirk Miller. She'd rather die alone than go through pain like this.

"I'm not trying to fix it," he said. "But I ... care for you and don't want you to be hurt."

"Too late, you jerk! If you 'cared for me' you'd be kissing me right now, not saying sorry."

"Ah, Kit." He half-laughed, half-groaned. He took a step closer to her, and she thought she might get her wish. She wasn't certain what kissing him again would do to her though, and she was scared he'd just reject her a third time, and it could possibly hurt worse than before. She didn't know that she could handle any more internal anguish than what he'd already caused today.

Gently, he brushed her long ponytail over her shoulder. Her flesh predictably tingled in response.

"Don't you feel that?" she demanded.

He smiled grimly and nodded, trailing his fingers up her neck. Kit moaned and leaned into his touch. Dirk cupped her jaw and stared at her with his impossibly blue eyes. Kit leaned closer. When they're mouths were inches apart, Dirk blinked as if waking from a deep sleep, and then murmured, "That's it. It's all just physical."

"Excuse me?" Kit snapped back to the reality of this guy being a jerk.

His hand dropped away, and he eased away from her then said again, "It's just physical. We don't even know each other."

Kit stared at him, too shocked and mad to even reply for a second, but then she found her tongue. "Just physical?" She'd given her soul to him at that waterfall, and he had the nerve to claim it was "just physical". "If you don't feel that this bond between us is so much more than physical, you're the hardest, coldest, piece of work I've ever met."

Dirk pressed his lips together and searched her gaze. Then a shutter went over his face, and he backed up another step. "Exactly, I am hard and cold and a 'piece of work'." He gave her a placating smile. "I've dated so many women, and I know you've got men 'crawling to your door step'. It doesn't matter to either of us if we walk away from this."

Kit thought it was a very good time to step in and slug him as hard as she could. She cried out in pain as her knuckles met his sculpted abs. He grunted and bent forward but didn't give her the satisfaction of crying out. Straightening, he asked, "Do you feel better?"

"No!" she yelled at him.

"Is your hand okay?"

She wanted to cradle her hand, but she straightened her shoulders and extended her fingers instead. "I'm fine. You aren't that tough."

He lifted his eyebrows.

"When I first met you, I thought you were the most confident, brave, handsome, and appealing man I'd ever seen."

Again, he gave her nothing but a slight flicker of a muscle in his jaw.

"Maybe it was your military background, maybe it came from a lifetime of being smart, good-looking, and successful, maybe it's just who you are. But right now, I think you're the most despicable and wimpy man I know."

He had the nerve to smirk at her, but she could see deep in his gaze that she'd struck a nerve. She jabbed a finger his direction, but didn't let herself poke him as her hand was still hurting, and she didn't need a jammed finger on top of everything else.

"You felt that power surge between us," she declared, "and you know as well as I do that it's not 'just physical'. But you're choosing to run away because of something ... maybe it's that you really are just a heartless jerk, but I don't think so. I think it's something to do with your father and your past."

At the mention of his father his shutter went up again. She wondered if he'd learned that in the military or learned it from his youth. Had his father abused him? Her stomach gave a violent turn, and she suddenly felt horrible for being so hard on him, for saying he was despicable and wimpy. He was the exact opposite, but she was hurting and had lashed out.

"Dirk," she softened her voice. "I'm sorry. Did your father ..." She swallowed and murmured, "Hurt you?"

Dirk's body went ramrod straight. She felt like she was watching an advertisement for military precision as his face appeared to be carved from granite. He didn't even give her a sarcastic smile as he said calmly and evenly, "No one has ever hurt me. And no one ever will."

He pivoted from her, checked that the bikes were secure, marched to his driver side door, slipped inside, and drove off. He didn't peel out or even drive fast. The calm way he left hurt her almost as much as him stepping away after that incredible kiss.

Kit stared after him, chills pinpricking on her skin. She'd let herself fall for a man who was cold, damaged, and didn't care for her at all. He claimed no one had ever hurt him or ever would. Well he'd hurt her enough for the both of them.

CHAPTER EIGHT

K it let the hot water pound her head and her body. Her tears drained away with the sweat from the bike ride, and she tried fruitlessly to shut her brain off. She could remember every beautiful touch and feeling from Dirk, and then just as quickly his cold rejection.

She put on one of the funny t-shirts Mae had bought her and some yoga pants. Brushing her hair out, she didn't bother with makeup. She glanced at herself in the mirror. Her eyes were swollen, and she looked awful. Her t-shirt read: *Fit-ish: Works out but definitely eats donuts*. She could use a dozen donuts about now, but the effort to go buy them wasn't worth the comfort food.

Ah, Mae, she missed her friend. At least Mae was happy and in love. That was more important than Kit being the same. Mae had been through so much and deserved every happiness with her dream man, Slade Steele.

Kit didn't know what to do with herself. It was almost five, so too late to work on finding a viable rental space or a loan for her new gym. She forced herself to get on her computer and put up some help wanted ads on the local classified pages, maybe that would appease that Colin guy for a few days. He hadn't bothered her since his initial phone call and email. Probably the type to expect his demands would be followed, only checking in to bring the hammer down.

Forcing herself to cut up some veggies and chicken, she cooked a simple meal, and then curled around her pillow and watched *The A-Team,* because she couldn't handle any chick flicks right now. Her brothers loved *The A-Team,* and they'd all watched it together years ago. It was her go-to when she wanted action and laughs, but Bradley Cooper as Face reminded her of Dirk: the bright blue eyes, the confidence, the charmer that every woman fell for.

Shutting the movie off, Kit punched her couch cushion and forced herself to put some socks and shoes on to go for a walk. The evening air was perfect, and she loved walking through her neighborhood of floating houses hearing music playing from one, laughter from another, the water lapping against them all. It was such a peaceful place. If only she had any peace inside. She stopped, bowed her head, and gave a prayer for help, right there on the dock.

Her phone rang and she yelped, "Thank you," to heaven then yanked it from her pocket. "Facetime call: Mae Delaney, soul sister," her phone chirped.

"Mae!" she screamed in her excitement.

"Kit!" Mae looked glowing, beautiful, but wore an interesting outfit: a pink t-shirt over the red and white polka-dotted dress Kit had put in her friend's suitcase for Mae's time with Slade. Before Kit could read the words on her t-shirt Mae thrust her left hand in front of the camera. "I'm engaged!"

"Oh my goodness, oh my goodness." Kit luckily found a bench to sink into. Happiness for her friend overwhelmed her. "How? When?"

Mae proceeded to gush out the perfect and adorable story of Slade asking her, with his brothers' and sister's help and some very funny t-shirts. When she read Mae's t-shirt, *Tough enough to bring a Steele to his knees*, Kit laughed and said, "Slade Steele is officially the smartest and luckiest man on the planet."

"He's heaven," Mae sighed happily, so in love she glowed.

"I'm seriously so happy right now," Kit said. The sun was setting to the west, and it was a glorious summer night. She was ecstatically happy, for Mae. Thank heavens this news could take the sting out of her anguish over the loser Dirk Miller.

"Me too." Mae lifted her ring finger again and squealed. "It's so big!"

Kit laughed. Mae was adorable but usually not overexcited. That was most often Kit's role. "It's gorgeous," Kit agreed. "Obviously Slade wanted to make sure no other man would dare look twice at you."

"Ha!" Mae laughed. "Obviously Slade has nothing to worry about. I'm so in love, Kit. I didn't know it was possible to be this happy."

"Oh, Mae, you deserve it. You're my favorite person ever, and Slade is incredibly lucky. I love you."

"I love you too." Mae paused and smiled at her but then said quickly, "Can you fly here tomorrow afternoon? Slade will send his jet."

"Why?" She could go on a quick trip. She didn't have classes or training Saturday or Sunday. She didn't want the pity invite, and though she longed to be with her best friend, Mae and Slade needed to be together, not have her as the third wheel.

"I just want you to share in this happiness, sweet friend. You would love Lottie, she's stinking adorable." Her voice lowered conspiratorially. "And Slade's brothers are almost as hot as him."

Kit's stomach filled with ice. She didn't want to flirt with any hot men. Clutching at her throat, she wondered what Dirk had done to her. She always wanted to flirt with hot men.

"You can have your pick—football star, military hero, extreme sports crazy man." Mae laughed. "Though Jex doesn't really appreciate it when you call him crazy. Anyway, you'll love all of them and Slade's parents. They're the best! It's like your family who just always loved and accepted me. Slade's family is like that. They'll adore you."

Why not? Maybe one of Slade's handsome and accomplished brothers would snap her out of her Dirk obsession. Maybe Dirk was right, and what they had between them was all physical, nothing special. And maybe bike shorts would actually look attractive on somebody besides Dirk Miller. She grunted in disgust.

"Kit? I lost you sweetie."

"Sorry." She wished she could spill the whole Dirk Miller saga and get Mae's advice and sympathy, but no way was she dampening Mae's happiness tonight. Someday soon her best friend could help and comfort her, but right now it was all about sweet Mae and smart, lucky Slade. "Of course, I'll come."

"Yes! Yes! Slade said he'll send you the time and coordinates. I think the plane will be there around one. I told him you'd need to fly back Sunday night so you can teach early Monday morning. I'm going to come back with you and try to get caught up on work stuff, and then Slade's going to fly there the end of next week. I get to show him the beauties of Sausalito and Muir Woods, and we've got to figure out, and soon, when and where we want to get married. Can you help me with the marriage junk, please, please, please? Slade's mom is awesome, but she doesn't know me well enough yet. She keeps saying she doesn't want to plan it all as it's my day, but I want to tell her, please plan it, I hate this crap." She blew out a breath. "Sorry. I'm getting ahead of myself."

Kit laughed. She'd missed her friend. "Of course, I'll help you."

"Yes! I love you. I've got to go. Time for more kissing on my much too handsome fiancé." She gave a very un-Mae-like squeal. "I love my life!"

"I love you."

The call ended, and Kit sat staring out at the water and lights reflecting in the bay as the sun had completely disappeared. Mae loved her life. Nothing was more important than that. Yet Mae's happiness did leave Kit very much alone. Even more so now that she had experienced bliss with the jerk Dirk and knew she'd never experience it again.

CHAPTER NINE

Dirk blinked at the weak light streaming through the open windows of his luxurious hotel room. He glanced over at the clock, seven-thirteen a.m. So, he had slept, at least a little bit. He'd spent most of yesterday afternoon berating himself for his callous treatment of Kit, and his complete inability to have a normal relationship, even with the most perfect woman for him he'd ever met. *Just physical?* He'd really said that to the most intriguing and sincere woman he knew, after the most amazing connection of his life. He was such a lying idiot.

He'd finally forced himself to turn the pity party soundtrack off and get to work about five o'clock last night. He'd worked until two a.m. and forced himself to lie down, but he'd tossed and turned.

Today was Saturday. He couldn't go find Kit at her gym and though he had her home address as her employer, she didn't know that. Why would she want him to turn up anyway? She'd given him every chance to confess that he'd never felt this unreal bond to and happiness with any human before. She'd waited for him to admit that if he had a heart to give, that heart would be hers. Little did she know, he didn't function emotionally. Well, he did have a charitable side and enjoyed doing kind things for employees, but he didn't have the ability, upbringing, time, or desire to form any lasting relationships.

For a short time when he was with Kit, he thought he might have something in common with his father besides business sense, that they were both the type who gave away his heart at the touch of a woman's lovely lips. Now he knew he'd been right all along, and he was exactly like his mother—cold and heartless, not caring who she hurt as she walked away. He knew he'd hurt Kit and how he loathed himself for it. He should just stay far away or tell her he'd bought her gym, he was now her demanding jerk of a boss. That would seal her hatred of him.

He passed a hand over his face and stood, downing a water bottle, brushing his teeth, and dressing in a tank top and shorts. A long run might help, but he truly doubted anything could get him out of this funk. He'd cradled heaven in his arms, kissed an angel. She'd responded, and despite the feisty things she'd said and punching him when she was mad, he knew that she cared deeply for him.

He growled deep in his throat and headed out the door. Starting at a jog, he headed toward the grounds of Fort Baker, trying to decide if he wanted to run across the Golden Gate Bridge to San Francisco and explore the Presidio and Golden Gate Park, or if he wanted to go through Sausalito and on the biking and jogging trail to Mill Valley where he'd biked with Kit yesterday. He didn't need any help dredging up and wallowing in the memories of yesterday, so he headed toward the bridge.

He was passing the children's park when he saw a group jogging toward the play equipment, two tall, blond men who looked familiar, one pushing a baby stroller, two beautiful, dark-haired ladies, and an absolutely gorgeous, blonde woman. Kit. Dirk stopped, staring at the group, his focus on Kit. They were all chatting and laughing. Stopping at the park, the man with the stroller handed out water bottles while one of the dark-haired ladies took a baby out of the stroller and headed over to the swings.

One of the blond men wrapped his arm around Kit's shoulder, and she pushed at him with her elbow. Her voice floated over as she hollered at him, "Get off! You're all sweaty and gross."

Everyone laughed, but the guy didn't get off as Kit had insisted. He pushed her head into his sweaty chest and chortled at his immature move. Dirk started forward. He was going to thrash that guy for manhandling Kit. And what kind of a weird situation was this? Kit hadn't refuted him two nights ago that she was on a date with both of these guys. Now there were two more women in the mix. Kit wouldn't be involved in something unsettling like ... dating two married men? She had too much light and goodness in her, but maybe these men had deluded all of these beautiful women. The guy reaching for Kit again didn't seem to know how to take no for an answer.

Kit dodged away from the man. Dirk was approaching fast. Kit noticed him, and her blue eyes widened.

"Dirk?" she said.

His jaw clenched as he thought of how he was going to fight her free. With his military expertise and strength honed from perfecting his body, he could take down both of these men. Kit didn't need to be part of this weird group. Had he driven her to this, because he'd hurt her yesterday? Yet she'd already been with these two guys at Sushi Sticks on a date.

Kit murmured something to the guy, and then jogged Dirk's direction. He stopped and waited for her, not trusting himself to be civil to those two men right now. One of the guys went with the remaining woman toward the other brunette and the baby giggling on the swings. The guy who'd manhandled Kit stood watching Dirk.

Kit looked amazing in a pink tank top and gray shorts with her long, blonde hair in a ponytail. "Dirk?" she asked as she approached, her voice wary. "What are you doing here?"

"I was heading out for a jog, and then I saw you."

"Heading out from where?"

He pointed back to his hotel. Her jaw dropped. "That place is over five hundred dollars a night."

Dirk rubbed at his jaw, hating the secrets and everything else between them. "What are you doing?"

"We just finished an early, long run across to the Presidio, through the park and back." Her voice was slightly belligerent as if he had no right to ask what she was doing.

"Look, it's none of my business, but what are you doing with those guys? Maybe I'm old fashioned, and I definitely wasn't raised to care about it, but I still hold to the sanctity of parenthood and marriage. You told me you were dating both of them, but it looks like they have wives, or at least girlfriends. One has a baby." He was getting more and more heated. How could Kit be part of a group like this?

Kit's eyebrows were arched high, and her mouth was in a thin line. "I don't think you have *any* right to tell me which relationships to be a part of."

Dirk reared back. She was right, of course, but it still made him sick. He stepped in closer and touched her arm. Warmth and desire flowed through him at the simple touch. She glanced down at his hand on her arm then back up at him. Her jaw got even tighter.

"I told you I care about you, Kit."

"You lost all opportunity to care about me yesterday afternoon," she flung back at him.

"Excuse me? Hands off, buddy." One of the men had approached them without Dirk even noticing. That wasn't like him. His military training had helped him be aware of and in control of every situation. Kit was making him not in control of anything, and it terrified him.

Dirk's eyebrows rose. "Excuse *me*. Kit is *not* dating a married man."

"Well, you're not dating me so what do you care?" Kit jutted out her chin. She looked so irresistibly appealing. How was he going to stay strong and detached?

"Kit." He pushed out a breath. He cared far too much for her, and if last night's misery was any indicator, maybe he needed to give dating her a chance. What would that do though besides let him fall deeper in love, and then when he walked away, as he surely would, it would hurt her even worse.

The guy stared at him for half a beat then threw back his head and laughed. "You thought ... my little Kitty-Kat was dating me?"

"*Your* little Kitty-Kat?" Dirk glanced at her. "You allow that?"

"No, but I can't get them to stop." Sighing, she finally admitted, "Dirk, this is my oldest brother Isaac." She pointed. "That's his baby Isabelle and his wife Cassandra, Jake my other brother, and his wife Marcy."

"Dirk Miller." He automatically extended his and shook Isaac's hand, relief rushing through him. "Your ... brothers?"

"Excuse us, Isaac," she ground out.

Isaac lifted his hands. "By all means, don't let me interrupt." His blue eyes glinted. "I like the look in your eyes, Kat. If a man finally got my Kitty-Kat to fall for him, I'm all over letting that happen."

"Shut it," she muttered to her brother. Then, she turned and marched away from both of them. Dirk inclined his chin to her brother and followed her.

They finally reached a shady and somewhat private spot by the trees, a short distance from the park. Dirk wanted to pull her close and never let her go, instead he asked, "Brothers?"

Kit looked chagrined. "I never said they weren't my brothers."

He drew in a long breath. "You never said they were." Not that he had any right to berate her for not being up front. "I've been ... eaten up with jealousy." That he could admit, that showed exactly how deep he was invested in Kit. He'd never had a reason to be jealous of anyone before.

She narrowed her eyes. "What right do you have to be jealous of anything I do? You rejected me hard yesterday, remember?"

"I remember," he said miserably. He should be running away from this situation and the insane bond he felt to a woman he hardly knew.

"Then stay away." She stalked past him.

Dirk should've done it, but he couldn't let her leave. He made the mistake of wrapping his hand around her smooth, toned arm to stop her. Kit pulled in a quick pop of air, stopped in her tracks, and whirled on him. "Don't touch me," she ground out.

Dirk blinked down at her and instead of listening, he stepped in closer, ran his hand up her arm and around to her upper back and used his other hand to cup her cheek. "I can't resist you," he admitted.

Kit's pulse was pounding so fast he could see it in her neck. "I can't handle the head games anymore, Dirk."

"I know. You're right. I'm sorry." He took a steadying breath and told himself to take his hands off of her. Instead of obeying himself, he bent down low and kissed her cheek. At least he hadn't gone for her lips or he'd be sunk. The softness of her cheek and the slight salty taste of her skin made his stomach swirl with heat. "I'm sorry," he whispered close to her ear. "You're completely irresistible to me."

Kit melted against him and Dirk knew he had no choice but to kiss her. He was falling for her, was that the worst thing in the world? No. It was beautiful and perfect because it was Kit. Hang his past, his insecurities, and his stupid parents who had messed him up emotionally. Couldn't he work through all of that to be with her? He'd hire any therapist, go through every hard conversation, and dredge up the pain of his upbringing. All he wanted was this woman to never leave his arms.

Kit stared into his eyes, her blue gaze bewitching him. She didn't say anything, but he knew: she'd give him a chance, she'd forgive him, for she had fallen as surely as he had.

"Kat?" It was her brother, Isaac was it? Curse the interruption but she actually had a relationship with her family, and Dirk didn't want to alienate her brother. He straightened and turned to face the man, but kept his arm around Kit's back. "Looks like you're ... good here?" Isaac's blue eyes twinkled as merrily as Santa Claus's. "We're going to head to breakfast. Do you both want to come?" He grinned.

Kit darted a glance at Dirk. Dirk swallowed, loving that she was tough, feisty, and independent, but she looked up at him, as if they could make a decision together.

"Can we take a rain check?" Dirk asked, hoping that was the right answer. Hoping there was a chance for a *we* and future time spent with her family.

Kit met his gaze and nodded slightly. Dirk wanted to punch a fist in the air. He'd messed it all up yesterday, and he was a mess inside, but Kit was willing to give him a shot.

"Sure, man." Isaac chuckled and backed away, jogging to the rest of the family.

They all waved goodbye, giving Dirk questioning glances, but they left Kit in his care as they jogged away. In his care? Could he really be entrusted with such a perfect person? Could he trust himself to not hurt her again? A cold, guttural voice in his head told him no, he'd ruin it all and hurt her even worse if he didn't push her away and run, now. He ignored that voice and turned to her.

She blinked up at him, vulnerable, uncertain, and so beautiful. All he wanted to do was claim her lips again, but he needed to apologize, to grovel. *To what end?* that chilly voice asked. *So you can destroy her?*

"Look here," she said. "I don't do the vulnerable woman crap."

He smiled. "I can see that."

"But ..." she bit at her lip, and it was all he could do to stop himself from kissing her. "I'm a wimp for you, Dirk Miller. Please don't hurt me again."

Dirk's stomach filled with ice and that awful voice was back, *You'll hurt her, of course you will. She doesn't even know your real name.* "Kit ..." The part that just wanted to kiss her begged him to stop, but some of the truth spilled out. He cared about her too much not to warn her. "I don't know how to promise that. As evidenced by yesterday, I'm a complete mess. I don't know how to navigate a healthy relationship. Maybe you should just walk away now." He was all in at this point and realized she'd have to be the one to walk, to reject him. Hopefully it would hurt her less if she did. It would destroy him, but that wasn't important to him. All that mattered was Kit's happiness.

She studied him. "Is there hope? Am I being insane and naïve to believe that my love could heal you or ..." Her body froze, and she gave him a weak smile. "Did the word love just slip out of my lips?"

Dirk's heart leapt at the suggestion of her loving him. Had anyone ever loved him? Melanie did before she died. His dad when he was younger, but Dirk had distanced himself from his father after Melanie's death. He'd pushed away the only person who truly loved him. He'd never known love from someone pure like Kit. He wanted her love, would do anything for it, but he wouldn't lie to her. "Kit ..." He swallowed. "I would do anything to love you, to be loved by you, but I have to be honest ..." Honest about what? He was hiding so many things from her, he didn't know where to start. "I don't know if I'm capable of a lasting relationship."

She nodded. "It's pretty obvious you've been hurt or neglected."

Dirk wanted to go throw some logs around or beat somebody in a fist fight or lift hundreds of pounds above his head to prove how manly he was, that nobody could hurt him and the neglect from his childhood didn't matter, but Kit was willing to talk to him, to throw the word love out there, to be vulnerable ... for him. Nobody had ever done that for him; truthfully, he'd never allowed it. Not since he'd lost his surrogate mom, Melanie, had he allowed anyone close.

All he could do was nod. He realized that he still had his hand planted on her lower back. The feeling he had when he touched her was almost as unreal as the emotional impact she had on him. "Yesterday, I lied about us being only physical."

"I know you did." There was no condemnation from her, only acceptance. "The thing I don't understand is why. You feel what I feel, right?"

He loved that she was exposing her heart to him, and he would force himself to try to do the same. "Like you're the sun, moon, and stars to me? Like the world is going to end if I can't be with you?" he asked. Wow, he was taking this being open far too seriously.

Kit's eyes looked suspiciously bright. She bit at her lip again.

"Please don't do that," he groaned.

"What?" she blinked up at him so innocent and beautiful.

"If you keep biting at your lip, I'm going to have to kiss you, and I don't know if I can physically ever stop kissing you again."

Kit smiled tremulously. "I'm all gross and sweaty from my run."

Dirk laughed. "You think that bothers me? I lived in the deserts of Afghanistan and Kuwait with some of the sweatiest men on this planet. Besides, you'd look gorgeous in a burlap sack."

Kit arched onto tiptoes and pressed her lips to his. Dirk knew he hadn't been exaggerating about any of the feelings he had for her. The world exploded into light and a joy he'd never imagined he could experience. He pulled her in tight and returned her kiss, hoping she knew that he loved her, though he didn't know if he'd ever be able to express it correctly. Curse his parents for stunting him emotionally, no it was more like they'd cauterized his ability to ever have a healthy, loving relationship. Could he ever be worthy of such innocence and beauty as Kit possessed? He doubted it, but he kept on kissing her anyway.

They kissed and held each other close, and he didn't care that her lips tasted salty and she wasn't all fixed up and perfect. She was perfect to him. The most perfect, desirable woman. She was out of his reach, far too good for him, but she didn't seem to feel that way. She'd said the word love to him.

"Come on, guys, this is a children's park," an irritated male voice said from much too close.

They broke apart, and Dirk smiled at the red tinge to Kit's cheeks. She was biting at her lip again, and he almost ignored the guy and kissed her longer this time.

"Excuse us," Dirk told the frustrated father, and then turned Kit with his arm. He took her hand, and they walked farther away from the park toward some of the fort's outbuildings. "Is this far enough away to start kissing again?" Dirk asked.

Kit smiled, but then her eyes turned serious. "So, what does all this mean? Will you let me in, Dirk? Do we have a chance?"

Heavy questions that he didn't have answers to. Still holding on to her hand, because he couldn't stand to sever the connection, he tried to be as honest as possible. Yet he couldn't be completely honest, or she would probably run away. "I want us to have a chance, Kit, but ... there are some things I need to share. Things I might never heal from." And then there was the little fact that he was her boss, and she knew him under a presumed name.

She nodded. "But you won't push me away?"

"I'll try not to." He held his breath. He wanted to promise that he wouldn't, but that would be a lie. Yet he hadn't told her the truth about who he really was. When should he drop that bomb? Maybe as they grew closer she could heal him, and then he could share that he owned her gym and Dirk wasn't his given name. They had a lot stacked against them.

Kit pursed her lips and finally said, "That's the best you've got for me?"

He wasn't good enough for her. He knew that. "I'll try with everything in me to be worthy of you, Kit."

"I didn't say you weren't worthy of me."

"I know you didn't, but it's true."

Kit stopped walking and pulled her hand free of his grasp. Dirk's heart seemed to stutter. She realized how unworthy he was. She was going to break him. He deserved it, but he wasn't ready. Just a little longer to bask in her light. If he thought there was someone in heaven who cared, he'd say a prayer pleading for her to give him any time she could. Maybe Melanie could help him from the other side.

Framing his face with her hands, Kit whispered, "You are worthy of me and so much more, Dirk Miller. I'm not asking you to prove your worthiness; I'm asking you to not push me away emotionally and to give *us* a chance. Can you do that?"

He loved everything she'd just said, but Dirk's body felt clammy and that chilly voice in his head was screaming that he couldn't possibly overcome his past and his demons. Yet she was so trusting and loving. Maybe her goodness alone could pull them through. Instead of telling her all his fears and trying to explain the mess he was, he said bravely, "I can." It was scarier than fighting insurgents without a weapon.

Kit smiled and kissed him tenderly. Then she pulled back and said, "I'm running home, and I'm going to shower. My address is 24 Liberty Dock. Come over at noon, and I'll make you lunch. Then, we'll see what happens from there." She winked all sassy and cute, and then she turned and ran away.

Dirk wanted to sprint after her and kiss her and confess everything. Instead he stood still and watched her beautiful form jog away. He was in love with Kit Abbott, and that was more terrifying than anything he'd faced in the military or throughout his entire messed-up life.

CHAPTER TEN

K it floated back to her floating house. Dirk hadn't admitted that he loved her, and she hated that he didn't feel worthy of her. She knew he had some serious issues stemming from something with his father, but he said he wouldn't push her away, and he'd give them a chance. It was enough. She could tell their path was going to be rocky and twisted, but she was a prayer and she'd pray hard, and with the Lord's help she and Dirk had a chance at least. She truly did love him. It was crazy to even think it with how little she knew about him, but she could no sooner deny how she felt than she could cut herself off from Mae or her family.

Showering, she took her time getting ready and whistled as she entered her small, sunny kitchen and started pulling out ingredients for orange chicken and ham-fried rice. She knew Dirk liked sushi, so she hoped he'd enjoy other Asian dishes. She turned on Imagine Dragons radio and danced around the kitchen as she worked. She was sautéing the chicken, thinking how Mae loved this recipe, when it hit her. She was supposed to fly to Boston and be with Mae and Slade. The plane was landing in San Francisco for her at one. Cripes! She didn't even have a number for Dirk to tell him what was happening and beg him to come early so they had more time together. Oh, no. Why did she have to leave him when she'd just found him?

Wait! She had that card he'd given her the first night they met at Sushi Sticks, but where had she put it? She tore into her bedroom and searched through several purses but couldn't find it. Glancing at the clock, her stomach dropped. It was eleven. She grabbed her cell phone and asked Siri to call Cavallo Point Hotel.

"Cavallo Point," a friendly voice greeted.

"Hi. I need to get a message to Dirk Miller. He's a guest there."

"One moment, please." There was a pause, then. "I'm sorry, ma'am. There's no Dirk Miller registered here."

Kit bit at her lip, her palms clammy. The meat was cooking too fast. She turned it down and stirred it, trying to figure out if Dirk had lied to her.

"Ma'am?"

"I apologize. I must have the wrong hotel."

"Can I help you with anything else?"

"No. Thank you." She dropped the phone onto the counter, stirred the veggies, and then cracked the eggs into the mixture. They were sizzling when she added the chopped ham. Her mind was going faster than the veggies and chicken were cooking. The chicken was done so she added the sauce, let it bubble, and then covered it and shut it off. Putting the cooked rice in with the rest of the mixture she added garlic and soy, stirred it all up, put the lid on and shut it off.

There was nothing to do but wait. And ask Dirk so many questions. But she needed to pack too. She'd promised Mae she'd come, and Slade's jet had already travelled most of the way across the country. She couldn't simply say, "Sorry, I've fallen in love, and he's a complicated, beautiful mess so I need you to turn your lovely jet around, send it back without me. Thanks anyway."

Hurrying to her room, she packed, and then rolled her suitcase to the door. She and Dirk could eat quickly, clean up, and then he could ride with her to the airport. It wasn't close to enough time or the visions she'd had of them snuggling on her outdoor couch and going on another hike to Cascade Falls or one of the bridge loops in Muir Woods. Now they'd have hardly any time and all she wanted was to be with Dirk. Yet there was a nagging voice in the back of her head asking why he'd lie about staying at Cavallo Point. Maybe the receptionist just wouldn't share because of security issues.

Noon was slowly approaching as she set the table with paper goods and ice water. Normally she'd do nicer dishes, but she'd have very little time for cleanup before she needed to catch an Uber to the private airport that was a fifteen-minute drive on a no-traffic day. Thinking of that, she pulled up her Uber app and scheduled the car. She could probably ask Dirk to drive her, but she didn't know how this was going to play out. Their relationship was so tenuous, it terrified her, but she'd fallen for him too hard and their bond was so special to her, she couldn't give it less than her all.

There was a rap on the door, and she placed a hand on her stomach to quell the happy nerves that sprung up. She hated that they'd have short time, and she was concerned about the hotel not having Dirk registered, but she could hardly wait to be with him again.

Flinging the door open, she drank him in for a second. He was so irresistibly handsome wearing a soft-looking, blue t-shirt and black Volcom shorts. His blue eyes swept over her and he sort of groaned, "Ah, Kit. Do you have to make me want you every second?"

"You're the only one I want wanting me." She smiled, and then bit at her lip.

"I told you not to do that," Dirk warned.

Kit laughed but he cut it off, crossing the threshold and sweeping her into his strong embrace. She wrapped her hands around his neck and held on. His mouth came down on hers, all worries and the rest of the world disappeared. Dirk's kiss was hungry, full of passion and a promise of them, a promise of happiness and love and simply being together through rough times and good times. He was fully committing, to her, she knew it as surely as she knew that she'd never been kissed by any man equal to this.

He pulled back and grinned at her. "That was amazing and you smell …" He bent low, his breath brushed her neck. "Good enough to nibble on."

She laughed, "The food or me?"

"You." He softly kissed her neck.

Kit closed her eyes and cradled his head against her neck. Bliss, ecstasy, love, forever, how did she explain the way he made her feel?

Glancing up at her, Dirk murmured, "So you're feeding me lunch, and then I get to kiss you the rest of the day?"

Kit had never heard such a brilliant plan but remembering what she had to do today made her frown.

Dirk straightened, and his brow wrinkled in concern. "Which part don't you like?"

"Oh, love." She kissed him soundly. "I love all of it, but I forgot I have to fly to Boston. Slade's plane will be here at one."

"Oh." His arms loosened around her, but at least he didn't let go. "How'd you forget you were flying to Boston?"

"Because you kiss me senseless." She tugged him inside and shut the door. "The food's all ready. Let's eat and I'll explain."

He followed her into her open kitchen and living area. The water sparkled beyond the open sliding glass doors. Glancing around, he whistled. "This place is amazing."

"Thank you. My grandparents refurbished it before gifting it to me." She loved the soft tans and wood accents but most of all the windows everywhere.

"Wow. That's generous of them."

She shrugged. "I'm the favorite, so ..."

Dirk chuckled. "And your brothers didn't mind?"

"No. They each got a million dollars to put toward their homes as well."

He nodded. "That's very generous of them."

"My dad's an only child, so they only had the three grandchildren. They claimed they needed the tax write-off. Sit." She pointed to her small table. "I'll bring the food over."

"Let me help you."

"No. Sit."

"Sassy." He arched an eyebrow. "I like it."

"You like everything about me."

"True." He obediently sat, and she brought the food over then sat close to him, clasped his hand, and waited. He looked at her expectantly. "I get to hold your hand while we eat?"

Her brow wrinkled at his misinterpretation. She wouldn't mind holding hands, always, but she'd meant for him to offer a prayer. She couldn't think of a meal she'd ever eaten without praying first. "Would you like to pray or me?"

"Um." His eyes had a deer in the headlights look. "Can you do it, please? I've never prayed in my life."

Kit felt like she'd been punched in the gut. What kind of a life had he lived to never have said a prayer? "Never?"

He shook his head. "I'm ... sorry?" He sounded confused but also almost belligerent.

"It's not your fault, I'm just shocked. Nobody in your family believes in a higher power?"

His jaw tightened, and he clung tighter to her hand. "Nope, we pretty much just focus on the almighty dollar, greed, lust, and selfishness."

Kit had absolutely no response to that. He was joking ... she thought. No, the look in his blue eyes was angry and defensive. Terror raced through her as she suddenly feared that this morning at Fort Baker and these past few minutes might be the happiest she and Dirk would see. He was going to pull away from her, no matter that he'd said he could give them a chance.

"Kit ..." His voice was low and remorseful. He released her hand and clenched his into a fist. "I tried to explain that I'm not worthy of you."

"Stop it." She grabbed both of his hands and smiled at him. "There will be none of that talk at my table."

A muscle worked in Dirk's jaw. He looked like a ferocious warrior, ready to run from her and go conquer the enemy, but he didn't pull away.

"It looks like you've been needing me in your life."

Dirk actually smiled then, his face softening. "You have no idea."

"Let me teach you how to pray. Then we can snarf down this food and you can ride with me to the airport."

"I'll do you one better."

"Oh?" She smiled, her insides lighting up at his decisive tone. She loved a confident man.

"You teach me how to pray, we eat your delicious food, and we'll go pick up a suitcase for me, because I'm not letting you out of my sight."

"You'd come with me to Boston?"

He nodded. "Please."

Kit leaned in and kissed him. His warm lips responded immediately, and all food, trips, and prayers were forgotten for a few wonderful minutes.

She forced herself to pull back, clasped his hands tight, and bowed her head. "Father in Heaven we love thee and are grateful for so many blessings, more blessings than we could've imagined." Dirk squeezed her hands tighter. "Please bless this food, please bless us as we travel, please bless our growing trust and love." Dirk's hands became a vice grip on hers. "Please bless Dirk can know of thee and thy love. Amen."

She opened her eyes to Dirk staring at her. He swallowed and murmured, "So that's how it's done?"

"There's no formula. You just talk to Him. He's your father, and he loves you."

Dirk's eyes darkened to a navy blue and filled with despair, but he didn't comment. He released her hands and gestured for her to serve herself first. Kit scooped food onto her plate and waited while he did the same, and then she tried to eat quickly.

"Where's the fire?" Dirk teased.

"If you're really flying to Boston with me, we've got to rush!" she said between mouthfuls, pulling out her phone to cancel the Uber.

"If it's a chartered plane it will wait for us." Dirk teased, but he ate quickly as well. They tossed their plates in the garbage. Kit covered the pots with Saran Wrap and shoved them in the fridge.

"No Tupperware?" he asked.

"The food will keep. We'll be back tomorrow night."

She hurried to the front door and reached for her suitcase, but Dirk took it from her. Opening the door, he held it for her. She locked up, made sure she had her purse and phone, and walked along the docks to the parking lot and his Audi. She kept sneaking glances at his handsome profile. This was really happening. Her and Dirk. She was so happy, but there were some warning bells. They weren't clanging loudly, but they were clanging. He had no relationship with Heavenly Father or possibly his earthly family, he'd lied to her about staying at Cavallo Point, he was a waiter who lived like a millionaire, and he seemed like a flight risk, at any minute he might spring away from her. Could she clasp him tightly enough to not lose him? Was Dirk like a skittish horse needing freedom that could never get used to a harness? Had she just compared herself to a harness?

He loaded her and the suitcase, and then climbed in, started the vehicle, and drove toward San Francisco. Kit kept staring at him.

"Do I have food on my face?" he asked, winking at her.

"No, you're perfect, as always."

He reached over and wrapped his fingers around hers. Bringing her hand back to his side of the vehicle, he rested their clasped hands on his muscled thigh. Her stomach swooped and got all warm and tingly. She wanted this, wanted him so much. *Please don't let this bubble of happiness pop,* she prayed silently.

"So why are we flying to Boston on Slade Steele's plane?" he asked, squeezing her hand gently.

"Do you remember Mae?"

"Your best friend? The reason you and I met? How could I ever forget how indebted I am to Mae?"

Kit grinned, her happiness tank just kept getting filled by him. "She and Slade got engaged last night."

"You're kidding me. That quick?" His voice held something she didn't like, as if it were absolute idiocy to fall in love and make a commitment fast. She'd basically admitted to him that she loved him; did he think she was presumptuous and silly?

"There's nothing wrong with quick," she rushed to say.

He lifted his shoulders but didn't comment.

"What's wrong with quick?"

Dirk glanced over at her. "What lasting thing happens quickly?"

"Excuse me?"

"Nothing worthwhile happens in the snap of your fingers. If you want something lasting you have to work for it and work hard."

Kit stared at him, her stomach churning. "Mae and Slade have known each other for two years."

"But they haven't dated for two weeks."

They pulled into Cavallo Point and Kit's frustration at him acting like Mae and Slade were some quick burning relationship and the obvious insinuation that he wasn't going to just surrender his heart quickly to her disappeared as she remembered. "Are you really staying here?"

He nodded. "Yes. Why do you ask?" Parking in the visitor spot, he released her hand and hit the engine button.

"I called earlier, to try to tell you I had to leave at one, and the guest services didn't have you registered as a guest."

"Oh." He nodded. "I'm registered under my business." He gave her a very forced smile. "Tax write-off."

Kit nodded as if she understood, but those warning bells were getting louder.

"Do you want to come in or wait?"

"I'll wait." She pulled her phone out of her purse. "I'll catch up on emails."

"Okay." He jumped out of the car and jogged toward the hotel.

Kit watched him go, but instead of doing anything with her phone she put her head back and closed her eyes, praying for discernment and faith. Something was wrong with Dirk, something that went deeper than not knowing how to pray, and she never in her life thought there could be something more sad than someone not knowing how to pray. Was she insane giving her heart away to him?

CHAPTER ELEVEN

Dirk was blowing it. He could feel it. As he got back into the Audi and drove with Kit to the airport, there was a change in the atmosphere of the vehicle. She was suspicious of him. Did she know he wasn't who he claimed to be? Was she upset that he thought quick relationships like the ones his dad had been in most of Dirk's adult life would just fizzle and die? Did she suspect something because the hotel didn't have a Dirk Miller registered? He could've told her to try Colin Johanson.

Maybe he was just nervous and acting off, and it was reflecting onto her. He tried to tell himself to relax so he didn't mess up the most pure, beautiful relationship he'd ever been a part of, would ever be a part of. He wanted it to last as long as it could, but was that just more selfishness and greed on his part? Take everything he could from Kit before she discovered who and what he was? She'd dump him then and no one would blame her, least of all him, but the last thing he ever wanted to do was hurt her. He'd hurt her yesterday and it had devastated him. He wanted to hold on to her and slowly build an incredible relationship, the kind he'd only seen on the big screen, but it was like holding on to a beautiful butterfly. He was terrified he'd only break her wings and damage her.

They parked at the private airport, and he got their luggage and walked with her to the white Cessna waiting on the Tarmac. It was a comfortable plane with decent speed. He preferred his Airbus, more spacious and luxurious. She cast a few sideways glances at him but didn't say much.

A pilot and stewardess were waiting for them. "Miss Abbott," the pilot greeted her warmly.

She gave him and the stewardess each a hug. "Long time, no see." She grinned at them.

"It's lovely to fly with you again. You brought a friend?" the pilot asked.

"Yes. This is Dirk Miller. My ... friend."

Dirk shook each of their hands, forcing an easy grin. Her friend. He was the one that had just bagged on quick relationships. What did he expect? That she introduce him as the love of her life, the future father of her children? His throat got tight as fear crept in. He couldn't be a father. That was a horrifying thought.

They boarded the plane. The stewardess got them drinks and offered food, but they both declined. The pilot and stewardess each disappeared into their spaces, and they were alone. Alone. An hour ago he would've been ecstatic to have Kit all to himself for a five-hour flight. Right now he didn't know what to say, where to start. Awkwardness settled between them, and he panicked that it was all falling apart.

No! He wasn't ready to lose her. But what did he expect? That cold voice yelled in his mind. He knew, he'd known since his dad had divorced Melanie, and then he'd had to watch his dad burn through wives that he could never be like him, hurting people because he was incapable of giving his heart away. To protect women from himself, he went to his current format of only one date, rarely kissing a girl. It stunk for him, but it kept them from handing over their hearts to get thrashed when he walked away.

He couldn't let an implosion happen with Kit. She was one in a million and the bond and sparks they both felt didn't happen for most of the world, at least as far as he'd known or experienced. Well, they seemed to happen for his father, but then the sparks dulled and disappeared, and his father succinctly moved on. Not him and Kit. He refused to be his father. He refused to let her go. There was only one solution. His heart raced, and his palms got sweaty. He tried to discreetly wipe his palms on his shorts, and then reached for her hand.

"Kit?"

She turned to him. Her blue eyes were so beautiful, and he loved her. He could admit that to himself. She gave him a small smile. "You okay?"

"No," he admitted. He wanted to spill it all, but he wasn't sure where to start. He thought of Mae and Slade and thought he could fix at least that wound. "I'm sorry I said what I did about Slade and Mae."

"That they rushed things?"

"Yes. I'm sure they're a great couple, and they'll be very happy."

She nodded, studying him. "It's not just about Slade and Mae though. You think ... we're moving too quick?"

Dirk took a shaky breath and admitted, "It terrifies me. I've never felt anything like this, and I don't want it to be like a match that strikes, and then burns out because there's no kindling or wood to support the fire. Does that make any sense?"

She turned toward him and tucked her legs underneath her in the recliner type chair. Dirk took this as a very good sign that she was getting comfortable and would talk things through with him, wouldn't retreat. If only he could be as certain that he wouldn't retreat. How much could he really share without showing her how truly un-grounded and messed up he was?

"It does, but we've both committed to giving us a chance. As long as we're both all in, we can build that kindling, find those long-burning logs, keep adding to our fire, right?"

Dirk felt a rush of emotion that was unfamiliar and scary to him, but it also felt really good, really right. "I like the way you think," he murmured, brushing her hair over her shoulder.

She grabbed his hand, pulled it to her lips and pressed a lingering kiss in his palm. "I just like you, Dirk Miller."

Dirk suddenly wished more than anything that she'd call him by his real name. He liked Dirk but he was Colin, and he wanted to hear it from her lips before he kissed her, after he kissed her. He could kiss her while she said it all breathy and beautiful.

"Dirk? Can you talk about it?"

"About?" he questioned, stalling. About his real name. Was it time to tell her? Would she hate him? No. This was Kit. She'd told him she liked him, told him she loved him. She was the most open and kind and perfect woman he'd ever met.

"Why you worry about rushed relationships? You were very ... adamantly opposed. We can take all the time we need, Dirk. I don't want to rush you. I just want to be with you."

Dirk could not stop himself as he leaned in and kissed her tenderly. Only military self-control allowed him to pull himself back and focus on the conversation. In order to not burn out quickly it couldn't all be physical. He'd lied and claimed they were just physical yesterday at the waterfall. Nothing could be further from the truth. Their physical connection was unreal, and he could happily waste years kissing her, not acquire another property, simply focus on being physical with Kit, but he wanted to develop the emotional connection and the trust too. Trust! What if she thought he'd lied to her when she found out he was her boss? He had lied, but not for nefarious reasons, right?

"Repeat the question, please," he murmured, still focused on her luscious lips.

Kit giggled then said, "Why do you have such an issue with a relationship that develops quickly?"

He nodded, held tightly to her hand, and reclined into the seat. He could tell her his real name soon, and then practice all that kissing with her calling him Colin, but right now he had to share with her about his past. He was terrified.

"My mom deserted us when I was eight," he started with.

"I'm sorry," she sounded like she meant it.

"It's fine. Well, it wasn't fine, and I pretty much hate what she's done to me, but ... okay it's not fine. She broke my dad and me. Later she got thrown in prison, which helped my dad protect me and our family money, but I ... I hate her. The day she left ..." He tried to force himself to let the memories come, go back to that dark place he never let himself go. For Kit. To help her understand. Would it help their fledgling relationship? Maybe. Sharing was important. At least he'd heard that in a college class or something. *Please don't let it tear us apart. Please don't let her realize how messed up I am.* He startled as he realized he was praying and that cold voice he'd heard earlier didn't even try to push its way in. He smiled. "You're rubbing off on me."

"What?" Her brow squiggled. He probably wasn't making any sense, jumping around from subject to subject.

"I think I just said a prayer in my mind."

She smiled softly. "About?"

"For us."

"I love that."

She didn't say any more, and he knew she was waiting patiently for his sad story. He studied the plush airplane, wondering how she'd respond when she found out he owned three jets. *Focus, man,* he chided himself. Kit obviously didn't care about money, her grandparents had given her a million dollar floating house, and she'd acted very nonchalant about it. Then he started worrying what his money might do to them. She'd fallen for him as a waiter. What if she hated rich guys for some reason? Maybe a rich guy had hurt her? He'd destroy anyone who hurt her. So, if he hurt her again, could he destroy himself?

"Dirk?" Her soft voice snapped him back to reality. "The day she left?"

He nodded and focused on their joined hands. "Can I hold you?" he asked quietly. It came out much too needy. He didn't know that he'd ever been needy before; always the tough guy, always in control. Not anymore. He was a complete wuss for Kit. With her, he was doing and saying things he never thought possible.

She didn't say anything, simply unbuckled her seatbelt as he unbuckled his. Anticipation to hold her close pushed away the anxiety about sharing his past. She sat sideways in his lap in the spacious reclining chair, and he cradled her close to his chest. Savoring the rightness, he wondered if he'd ever get complacent about touching her. He hoped not.

He trailed his fingertips along her back and tried to spit it out quickly. The scant memories of the one person he rarely let himself think about. "My mom was always distant, never one to hug or be there or say, 'I love you'. My dad tried to explain when I left for college that it wasn't me, she'd been addicted to painkillers since shortly after my birth when she'd had a c-section, and then ripped her ACL running while trying to lose the baby weight and tripped on a curb. Too many prescription drugs too close together, and she became an addict."

"He didn't explain that until you left for college?" she asked.

"Yeah. My dad ... He loves me, I know he does, but he doesn't deal with emotional stuff either, and he flits from one woman to the next. To be honest I haven't had much respect for him the past eight years. To him life is about making more money and finding his next wife."

She was getting an earful already and probably wondering if Dirk was stable emotionally. He wasn't. Would she leave him when she discovered it? Why was he telling her all of this, digging his own shallow grave?

"How many times has he been married?"

Instead of pulling away from him, she rested her hand on his chest and looked up at him so sweetly, so innocently. *Please don't let that look fade away*, he begged whatever higher power would listen. The praying thing was actually kind of comforting. Odd.

"We're on wife eight. Tracy. Pretty sure she's my age."

"So as a child and teenager your mom was gone, and your dad kept marrying different women?"

He shook his head. "He didn't start burning through wives until after Melanie died. She was his second wife, and I loved her." He kept rubbing Kit's back as he talked. "It took Dad a while to heal after my mom left. He dated Melanie for almost two years before marrying her when I turned fifteen. She was so feisty and funny. She took my teenage mood swings in stride, and she seriously loved me. She thought I could do no wrong. Have you ever been around somebody like that? Who just thinks you're the best thing since the Humvee?"

"Always the military man." Kit smiled. "My mom's like that and my friend Mae."

"I'm glad. I'm sure everybody thinks you're the best thing because you are."

She laughed. "You are too."

He shook his head but didn't refute her statement. She'd know soon enough.

"What happened to Melanie?"

Dirk pulled Kit in tighter, taking solace, strength, and joy from holding her in his arms. Was he only a taker, like his father? He hoped he was giving those same things back to Kit, but if he hurt her, if he let her fall for him when he knew he was an emotional mess, unworthy to even be close to her, didn't that make him worse than his father?

"Dad divorced her when I was twenty-three. It was his longest marriage, besides my mom. Since then he's only stuck with a woman for a year or so. I was in Afghanistan, deployed with the Navy." He paused and sniffled. Horror raced through him. He wasn't a sniffler. He composed himself, tried to recite the facts coldly, detached, the way he'd lived his life.

He would've been able to pull back into his chilly box, but Kit touched his face and gently tilted it down until he met her teal blue gaze. "It means so much to me that you'll share, but if it's too hard I understand."

"Ah, Kit." He kissed her, long and thoroughly. His body heated up having her so close. This was the first kiss they'd had snuggled in a compromising position. He forced himself to pull back. He would never take advantage of her. He'd always been in control of himself that way, and he wasn't about to slip with the most amazing woman he'd ever met.

Dirk stroked her cheek and finished the story, "Melanie loved my dad as much or more than she loved me. Apparently, the day the divorce was final, she got drunk, and drove her Porsche off a cliff into the ocean."

Kit popped out a breath as if he'd punched her. "No!"

He nodded. Now that it was all spilling out he actually wanted to tell her. Kit seemed to care so much, when nobody had ever cared about his story before. Not that he'd ever let anybody get close enough to ask. He'd become an expert, from childhood on up, at drawing other people out, making them feel good, getting their story. Everyone seemed to like him, and he was pronounced "charming, caring, and intriguing" by many news outlets. No one knew what he was hiding. Except for Kit.

"It was worse than losing my own mom," he admitted. "My dad was worried I'd turn to alcohol or drugs, but that was what had taken the two women I loved away. I would never be that weak. So, I just worked harder. I pushed myself physically to be in ideal shape, I pushed myself in business to be successful, and I pushed myself socially to be everybody's friend, but I never let anybody get close."

She nodded. "That makes sense. From the moment I met you, I thought you were a charming player, but you were hiding so much."

"Only you could dig to the bottom of it."

They sat in silence for a few seconds, and Dirk wondered if she'd start questioning him about business. She'd said something a few days ago about him going to Harvard and then becoming a waiter. She probably assumed, now, that was part of his going off the deep end after Melanie had been killed, but if she listened she'd notice he said he was successful at business. She probably already knew that as well; from the vehicle he drove, the hotel he stayed at, and the bikes he'd claimed to rent. Nobody rented Trek Emondas out. He waited for the questions, ready and willing to spill all. What she asked wasn't where he wanted to focus right now.

"You started telling me about the day your mom left. Do you feel comfortable sharing that?"

Dirk's eyebrows lifted up. He was thrown back to the dark hole. "My mom, I think she tried. I always assumed she was so flaky, annoyed, and cold because there was something wrong with me, but I understand, logically at least, that it was the drugs. It was shortly after I turned eight. She'd forgotten my birthday. My dad tried to make up for it. He took me on a plane ride to Catalina Island. We rode a golf cart all over, and he was happy and fun. He took me to lunch, and we collected shells on the beach. It was a good day, but it still hurt that my mom hadn't even said, 'happy birthday' or wanted to come with us."

"A few days later she was actually awake when I went to school. She told me she was going to pick me up from school, and we were going to get pizza. I could have a whole pepperoni pizza to myself. I can still remember how happy I was all day, so excited, my mom and a pizza all to myself."

He glanced down at Kit, her blue eyes were bright, and a tear crested her eyelid. He gently wiped it away. "Don't cry for me, Kit."

"I can't help it." More tears spilled over. She reached up and clung to his neck, burying her face in his neck. "She didn't come, did she?" she murmured against his neck, sniffling.

"No," he murmured.

"How long did you sit there?"

"I don't know. It felt like forever but maybe half an hour. The secretary finally called my dad. He dropped everything and came, took me for pizza, and ordered me my own pepperoni. He pretended like everything was okay, but every few minutes he'd try to call her again. He finally got her to answer her phone while we waited. I can still remember him yelling at her, my dad never yelled, and it terrified me. When he hung up, he didn't even have to admit it to me. I knew. She'd left us. I knew it when I sat at that school waiting. The haunted look in my dad's eyes confirmed my every fear. She wasn't coming back." He felt it all over again, the despair, the pain; eventually the ability to coldly shut himself off like his mom had taught him by example. "The pizza came then. I couldn't eat any of it. I hate pizza."

"Oh, Dirk." She softly kissed his neck, and then she simply clung to him. He could feel her tears on his neck. He didn't cry himself, he hadn't cried since that day at the pizza parlour, but he wished he knew how to express what it meant that she would cry for him.

He reclined the seat and leaned back, getting comfortable with her in his arms.

"Are you okay?" she asked quietly.

"It feels good to share it. To trust someone with my past. Thank you." He meant it. He'd never trusted anyone like he trusted her.

If only he could trust her with all his secrets. It was definitely past time for that.

"You've never told anyone?"

He shook his head. "I'm too tough to share." He gave her what he hoped was a charming grin.

"You are tough and brave and handsome and irresistible."

Dirk's stomach swirled with heat at the way she was looking at him. She didn't look at him like he was damaged goods. She looked at him like he was the most appealing man she'd ever met. How could Kit be so perfect for him? How could she love him so unconditionally? He knew he needed to share the other secrets, but first he was going to let himself take advantage of her lovely mouth. He kissed her and savored every second of the connection.

She was the one who broke the kiss, and they were both panting for air. Snuggling down into the seat next to him, she murmured, "Maybe we better slow things down."

"Smart girl." He kissed her forehead, his mind and body racing with heat for her.

She glanced up at him. "As a Christian, I've kept myself pure for marriage."

The heat fled but something deeper replaced it. He kissed her forehead again. "That's why you shine so bright, Kit. You're the most beautiful woman, ever." He cleared his throat and admitted, "I've never been with a woman."

"Truly?" She glanced quickly up at him, her eyes filled with hope. "Not that I'd blame you or judge you if you had."

He smiled. "You'd never judge anyone. I love that about you. Truly I haven't. My dad, as far as I know, has never had sex outside of marriage, and he taught me as a teenager to do the same. The way he's flitted from woman to woman, especially after Melanie ... it sickened me, and I promised myself I'd never be with a woman like that until I found someone I could trust and love. I didn't know if that was truly possible, or just a pipe dream, until I met you."

Kit blinked up at him. "I love you, Dirk."

He wanted to say it back. Terror rushed through him, sweat popped out on his brow. *I love you. Say the words, you jerk.* He opened his mouth, and she smiled so sweetly at him. Dirk wimped out and kissed her instead, pouring his heart and soul into the kiss. Couldn't she feel how much he loved her? He prayed she could, that she wouldn't dump him before he could say those three words.

They finally had to catch a breath and instead of reprimanding him or demanding he say he loved her, Kit kept smiling sweetly at him. Then she rested her head against his shoulder and murmured, "I'm exhausted. I couldn't sleep last night."

Dirk laughed uneasily. "Neither could I, stewing over how I'd messed up with the most incredible woman in the world."

"You did mess it up." She cuddled closer. "But you've redeemed yourself pretty nicely." Yawning, she rested her hand on his chest and closed her eyes.

"Rest," he whispered. "We have plenty of time to talk." It was a relief to have a break from sharing, from knowing he needed to tell her he loved her, and reveal who he really was.

"Okay." She was breathing evenly and deeply within seconds.

Dirk reveled in the feel of her close and hoped he was telling the truth. He hoped they had all the time in the world to talk, but he was still worried it was all going to become cold pizza, the crust and cheese hardening with the stale smell making his stomach churn.

CHAPTER TWELVE

"Kit? Kit?" She stirred to Dirk's deep voice and glanced up into his handsome face. "We need to get buckled in for landing."

Kit straightened and saw the flight attendant watching them with a smile. "Sorry. Dirk said you're exhausted."

"Yeah, it's his fault I didn't sleep last night." As the attendant's eyebrows arched, Kit realized how that came out, and her face flared with heat. "I mean ..."

"It's okay. You don't have to explain it." She held up a hand. "We'll land in about fifteen minutes. If you'll please buckle up."

Kit nodded and climbed into her own seat, ignoring Dirk's deep laughter.

"That did not come out right," she muttered.

"It's a great mental image for me, though."

"Stop it, you."

He took her hand and didn't hide his smile. Kit felt groggy as they landed and disembarked. She was sure she looked a mess, but Dirk held her hand and treated her like she was a priceless treasure. He loved her. He hadn't voiced it, but his kiss and his look said it all. She could wait patiently for the actual words. Maybe their every dream of being together could come true.

They both took in the sights as they drove to Slade's parents' house, not talking much but enjoying being close. Kit appreciated everything he'd shared with her, and prayed he wasn't too damaged from his parents to form a lasting relationship. She'd been raised in such a happy, loving home, but she knew from her experiences with Mae losing her entire family at fourteen that it could really mess a person up emotionally and make it hard to form lasting relationships. She liked to think she and her family had helped Mae, and now Mae was happy with Slade. She'd never loved someone like she loved Dirk. She'd work hard to keep adding kindling and logs to their fire. As long as they were both committed, they could make it work.

Slade's driver pulled up to a gorgeous Cape Cod style house right on the beach. It was south of Boston, but she wasn't sure how far south. It was so beautiful here, the temperature a perfect seventy-five on this summer evening. Kit was excited to see Mae and wondered what she'd think about her bringing Dirk along. Her friend knew nothing about Dirk and Kit being together. That was crazy as Mae usually knew everything about Kit's life. Actually, Mae had lived vicariously through Kit's dating life for a long time until Slade found her, the smart man.

Dirk slid out and held the door for her. They both thanked the driver and Dirk palmed him some money. The driver climbed back into the vehicle. Kit appreciated all Dirk shared with her, but there was still something missing. The casual way he took in a private jet, tipping the driver like he did it every day, talking about his successful business, no shock over how unreal this house was. She opened her mouth to ask him about it, but Dirk smiled down at her and stole a quick kiss. "You look so beautiful," he murmured against her lips.

She melted into him, arching up to kiss him again.

"Are you Cinderella?" A sweet voice demanded from beside them.

Kit whirled to face a gorgeous, teenage girl who had the distinct almond-shaped eyes of someone with Down syndrome. Slade stood next to her and ... "Mae!" she screamed, flinging herself against her friend.

They hugged and hugged. She pulled back and framed Mae's face. "Is he treating you like an angel, or do I need to cut his ears off?"

Mae laughed happily.

"Of course my Slade treats her right," the teenage girl said. "I Lottie. Are you Cinderella and Prince Charming? You both have the blue eyes and are so pretty."

They all laughed.

"Nice to meet you, Lottie," Dirk said, reaching out his hand.

She took it but didn't shake it, holding it instead and batting her eyelashes. "You're very handsome, Prince Charming."

Dirk smiled. "And you are very beautiful."

"Can I be your princess or do you like Cinderella better?"

Dirk let Lottie hold on to his hand, but he wrapped his other arm around Kit again. Lowering his voice to a stage whisper, he said, "I wish you could be my princess, but the thing is ... I actually love Cinderella."

Kit's heart stuttered then seemed to expand. He'd actually said it. She smiled and felt her eyes grow bright with emotion.

"What?" Mae exploded. "I only introduced you two last week!"

Lottie released Dirk's hand with a harrumph but was instantly smiling. "Young love," she sighed dramatically. "Who can guess at it?"

Kit wasn't sure what movie she was quoting, maybe a mixture of Disney's Robin Hood and something else. She wished she was alone with Dirk to tell him over and over again that she loved him and to hear him say it in his deep, throaty voice. Oh, how she loved him.

Lottie fluffed Kit's long hair. "You're very beautiful, Cinderella. I will concede this prince to you."

Everybody but Mae was laughing. Slade and Dirk shook hands.

"It's good to see you again," Slade said.

"You too." Dirk seemed a little uneasy to Kit. Was it because Mae was staring at both of them like they were nuts? "I apologize for coming uninvited," Dirk continued. "I couldn't stand to let her out of my sight."

"I understand how that goes," Slade said, winking at Mae.

"You stop trying to distract me," Mae threatened Slade. "How did you fall in love in a matter of days? You never let yourself fall for anyone!"

Kit smiled up at Dirk. "When he touches me it's like fireworks exploding."

"But that's just a physical reaction," Mae protested.

Dirk and Kit both laughed at that. He squeezed her waist. "It's so much more than physical," he murmured in her ear.

Kit felt warm all over. She loved him, and he truly loved her back.

"I'm sorry," Mae said. "It's nothing against you ..."

"Dirk," Kit supplied.

"I'm just in shock. Kit goes through men faster than I can drink a Diet Coke, and she never, ever gives her heart away."

"I'm in shock too." Dirk looked deeply into her eyes, his own blue eyes full of wonder and happiness. "I have no clue how I got so lucky."

Kit grinned and threw her arms around his neck, kissing him soundly.

"Go, Cinderella, go," Lottie cheered, clapping her hands together then waving them at her forehead.

A well-built man strode out of the front door and down the porch. He looked a lot like Slade with dark coloring and a short beard. He was thicker than Slade and not quite as tall.

"Gunner." Slade gestured him over. "This is Mae's best friend Kit."

He shook Kit's hand. "Nice to meet you." Turning to Dirk before Slade could introduce him, Gunner said, "Colin Miller. It's a pleasure to meet you, sir."

Dirk's body tensed against hers. Everyone but he and Gunner looked confused. Gunner looked honored and Dirk looked ... terrified. Kit had no clue what to think. Was Dirk's first name Colin? The name he used in the military, maybe. He was reacting really oddly. Colin? Where had she heard that name recently?

"This guy is a Navy legend," Gunner continued, his voice full of respect. "Awarded the Navy Cross. Saved an entire platoon in a skirmish in Kuwait. Got his master's degree from Harvard online while he was deployed in Afghanistan. Then he became the youngest billionaire in history and retired from active duty. It's truly an honor." Gunner sort of bowed to him.

Dirk was a billionaire? She'd suspected he was wealthy from whatever his "side business" was and he'd said something on the plane about family money. Yet, the youngest billionaire in history? What else was he hiding?

"That's why I recognized you that first night at the sushi place," Slade said. "I've read all about you and your businesses. Miller International, right? I can't believe I didn't piece it together faster. Why were you posing as a waiter?"

Posing as a waiter? What was happening here? She stared at Dirk not sure who she was seeing.

Dirk laughed uneasily. "Most people see what they want to see. I buy up small businesses and usually play an undercover boss of sorts for a few weeks then fix problems and reward employees who deserve it."

Slade nodded his approval. "Interesting."

"I enjoy it." Dirk shrugged.

Lottie had wandered away to pick flowers, obviously bored with the conversation. Mae's gaze was swiveling back and forth between Kit and Dirk as if she sensed something was wrong. Kit's brain was spinning, but she wasn't sure why she felt claustrophobic and upset. Dirk wasn't the person he'd portrayed. He was a billionaire who played undercover boss. Boss? Buying up small businesses? No! She felt suddenly chilled, embarrassed, and disjointed.

"C-colin?" she managed to get out. No way. This couldn't be happening.

Dirk clung to her waist, staring down at her, his blue eyes begging her. Begging for what? "That's my given name," he murmured.

She swallowed hard but managed to get out. "Colin Johanson?"

Dirk closed his eyes then refocused on her. "That's the name I use for business transactions sometimes."

Kit ripped herself away from his grasp and wrapped her arms tightly against her chest. "Business transactions? You're the jerky boss who wants me to change everything." He clenched his fist, but didn't respond. "So that's what I am to you, a business transaction?"

"Never, Kit. Please don't do this. I fell in love with you."

"Don't you talk about love with me," she yelled at him, horror racing through her. She'd fallen so hard for him, and he'd been lying to her. Had he been laughing to himself the entire time? What had she done? How could she have been so stupid? She'd known he was a player from their first interaction, and she'd known there was something off all along, but she'd let herself trust in her physical and emotional reaction to him, trust him.

"Please, Kit. Don't do this." He reached out a hand to her.

She batted it away. "Don't do this? What am I doing? From where I'm standing, you're the one who did everything to me. You lied to me. Why would you do that? How could you do that?"

Dirk opened his mouth, but she was just getting started. "Was everything a lie? Pretending to love me for your undercover boss ploy? Is that all part of your 'rewarding employees who deserve it' plan? Wow. How did I get so lucky?"

"No. This has never happened to me before. Give me a chance to explain."

"You used me," she hurled at him, her body chilled and disjointed. "Did you lie about your mom, too? Melanie?"

Dirk's jaw became iron. "Don't go there."

Lottie tapped Kit's arm. She pried her gaze from Dirk and focused on the young girl. "I don't think Cinderella is supposed to yell at Prince Charming. Save that for the ugly stepsisters."

Kit bit at her lip, feeling like a complete fool, with witnesses to boot. Why had she fallen so quickly without knowing who or what he was? "I'm sorry, Lottie, but he's not my prince."

Lottie's eyes widened. "Now you just being mean. He's your prince, you're meant to be, I can tell it."

Slade put his arm around Lottie. "We probably should go inside and let these two talk this out. Are you okay with that?" Slade asked Kit.

Kit wasn't okay with anything at the moment, but she didn't need Slade and his family watching her melt down, and she could handle Dirk, or Colin. Her heart was cracking inside her, no it was shattering. How could the man she thought she'd loved do this to her? Lie to her and make her fall for him under a pretense? A waiter. She snorted in disgust.

Slade, Gunner, and Lottie turned toward the house. Mae stormed up to Dirk. "You hurt her, and I'll cut your ears off," she threatened. Mae was barely five-five. Dirk towered over her at six-three, and he was twice as thick as her with his ropey muscles. Kit might have laughed at the threat she'd recently teased Slade with, but she was too angry and hurt and confused.

"Cut them off," Kit said snidely.

Mae shook her finger at him. "Watch it. My fiancé will beat you up." She hurried to Kit and hugged her. "I can stay with you," she whispered.

Kit loved Mae's devotion to her. "It's okay." Her eyes flickered to Dirk. "I can handle him." He'd never hurt her physically, but he'd devastated her emotionally. She was ticked at him for it. A little voice said that he'd tried to warn her, but she hadn't listened, plowed right ahead and given him everything.

Mae gave Dirk one more glare before slowly going into the house. Kit was suddenly drained. She didn't want to fight with Dirk. She just wanted him to leave, and she wished she could go home and have a proper cry, but it wasn't to be. She'd have to face Slade and his family. Gunner Steele, who apparently idealized Dirk, Preston, the Patriots' football player, and Jex, the famous extreme sports guy. But none of that mattered to her right now. How could Dirk have lied to her face time and time again?

His footsteps slowly approached. "Kit," he whispered in that deep, throaty voice that she loved. No, she didn't love it. The conversation she'd had with her jerk of a new boss not long ago replayed in her mind. Dirk's voice. Colin Johanson. She'd tried to Google him that first day he'd called but she hadn't found anything that seemed to fit, same thing with Dirk Miller. When she first met him, she'd attempted to Google him but no matches to Dirk's face.

Colin Miller. The name fit him, but he'd always be Dirk to her.

She took a steadying breath and made herself face him. As she looked into his blue eyes, begging her to understand, to listen to him, she almost gave in to the overwhelming desire to go to him, to hold him. What part of the things they'd shared was true and what were lies? How would she muddle through it to know? She couldn't trust Dirk to tell her the truth.

"Why?" she forced out. "Why did you lie to me?"

He spread his hands. "I do undercover boss with almost all my new acquisitions. It wasn't about lying to you."

She stared at him. "So, I'm just an acquisition now."

"Kit." He shook his head. "You know that's not how I feel."

"I don't know anything." She was hugging her arms to her chest so tightly her neck hurt. Her head hurt from lack of sleep and trying to reason out the past few minutes. But her heart hurt the worst. She'd fallen so deeply for Dirk, and he wasn't even Dirk. "I don't even know who you are."

"Give me a chance to show you."

She'd known from the start that Dirk had an inborn, unquenchable confidence. It had drawn her in initially and when she'd found out recently that he was also humble and had been through so much, she'd thought he was just about perfect. Sure, he had issues and a past but didn't everybody? Now that confidence and the fact that she didn't know if he was humble or which part of his story was true, made her irritable and angry. She felt completely out of sorts and irrational. It could be lack of sleep from last night, but she thought it more likely due to her heart being shredded, and she didn't know how to react.

"I can't," she responded miserably.

Dirk backed away. "I'm sorry, Kit," he said. He looked and sounded almost as miserable as she felt. She didn't think anybody could be as miserable as she was. "I tried to tell you that I wasn't worthy of you, that I'd mess it all up."

Kit's mouth opened. She wanted to tell him he was wrong, that he was worthy of her and she still loved him, but the pain of him lying to her while making her fall for him stopped her tongue.

She couldn't look at him any longer, or she'd forget his lies and beg him to still love her. She forced herself to spin and walk to the house. Every step away from him was harder than the last. As she reached the porch, she let herself glance back. Dirk hadn't moved, and she wondered if she was wrong. He looked every bit as miserable as she felt, but she couldn't go to him. Only time would heal this pain and hopefully give her some insight into what direction to go.

She pushed through the front door and let the tears spill over. As she noticed the entire family waiting expectantly for her, she tried to stop the tears, but she couldn't. Mae rushed to her, throwing her arms around her and holding her close.

"It's okay, let it out. It'll all be okay," Mae soothed her.

Kit clung to her friend but knew she was wrong. Nothing would be okay without Dirk.

CHAPTER THIRTEEN

K it made it through the weekend with Mae, Slade, and Slade's family. They were all fabulous people, not one of them referenced her break down or Dirk, rather Colin Miller. Except for Lottie asking a few times why Prince Charming left and why Kit had been mean to him. Kit didn't blame the sweet girl, but her Prince Charming was definitely gone.

They had a nice dinner Saturday night then stayed up late playing card games, laughing, and chatting. Kit did her best to be present. She'd hoped to be alone with Mae that night and talk everything out, but Lottie insisted on a sleepover in her room and neither she nor Mae could tell the darling girl no.

They went to church Sunday morning. After brunch, Preston chartered a boat and they went out sailing. The Steele's were an impressive family, and Kit loved seeing Mae at their center, beaming with happiness and love. Kit kept her distance from the handsome brothers, but she became fast friends with Lottie, even though the sweet girl kept reminding her that she needed to be nicer to Prince Charming when he came over again.

Prince Charming. Dirk couldn't be her Prince Charming. He wasn't even Dirk. She kept forcing him out of her mind, and he kept sneaking back in. Little things he'd said or did, the comfortable way they talked and teased, the unreal bond between them, the way it felt when they kissed. The depth of what he'd shared with her. Him admitting to Lottie that he loved her. Argh! She didn't know what to dwell on or push out, what to believe anymore.

Sunday, as she and Mae boarded the jet, she sank into the seat and closed her eyes so she didn't intrude on Mae and Slade whispering loving goodbyes and kissing just outside.

Mae finally floated onto the plane. They were in the air before Mae stopped grinning and clasped her hand. "Tell me all friend, please."

Kit shook her head, hating that she was tainting Mae's happiness but knowing Mae had to be here for her, just as Kit would always be there for her best friend. "I don't know where to start."

Mae stared at her with her dark eyes full of wonder. "I didn't think you'd ever fall in love."

Kit banged her head back against the cushioned seat. "Yeah, and look where it got me."

"Where are you, friend?"

"In misery." Kit sniffled, blinking the tears away and willing herself to stay in control. She hadn't cried again since she walked away from Dirk yesterday. Normally she'd never get teary eyed, but who could blame her? Dirk had hurt her, destroyed her, but she missed him so horribly she could hardly stand to think of another day passing without being near him.

Mae wrapped her arm around Kit's shoulder. "Have a good cry, sweet friend. I'm here."

Kit let out a choking sob, and the story spilled out between sobs, sniffles, and the cute stewardess bringing them chocolate and Diet Coke before disappearing again. Mae was staunchly on Kit's side, but she did remind Kit that she, herself, kept things from Slade, and he'd instantly forgiven her. This was so different though, but Kit kept wondering if she'd been too harsh on Dirk. The distance between them already felt too far to bridge.

When they landed, Kit felt marginally better, but she knew no one but Dirk could ever make her feel truly happy again.

K it rose early the next morning and put on a cheerful face for her friends at the gym. Dirk, or Colin, Miller was not going to ruin her happiness. She was too strong and determined to let someone have power over her like that. She chose to be happy. That's what her mom taught her. But she could still ache for him and know that no one could ever get to her like he had. That was for the best though. If anyone ever got to her like that again, she might as well give up on finding joy in life. Niggling in the back of her mind was the hope that maybe he would come for her, maybe she could drop her pride and her pain, and they could sort it all out. Hope was a vicious friend sometimes.

As her nine a.m. class ended and filtered out, a man marched in wearing a suit and tie. She didn't have any personal training appointments until tomorrow afternoon. She'd half-wondered what would happen to her gym now. Should she be trying to start her own gym or simply look for another job? She didn't want to be at Colin Miller's mercy any longer. She wanted to be in his arms, but that was a completely different story and not a place she let herself imagine very often, only every other minute.

"Katherine Abbott?" the man said all crisp and lawyer-ey.

"Yes?"

"How do you do, ma'am? I'm here as one of Colin Miller's personal legal representatives."

"So you're Dirk's, I mean Colin's, lawyer?"

"Yes, ma'am."

Well that didn't take long. Monday morning and already time to face the music. Was she going to be fired or told she needed to get in line with his stipulations? She still had plenty of time before the deadline he'd given her, but he was probably all cold and analytical in his billion-dollar high rise or mansion on a cliff or wherever he lived when he wasn't pretending some under-cover boss lie.

"I'd like you to look over these papers, and then if they are to your satisfaction, you can sign and make the transfer of property and ownership of Bay Fitness possible."

"Excuse me? Did you say transfer? I never had any ownership. Joe's the one you need." She turned her back, proud of the composure she'd shown but not sure how much longer she could keep it up.

"I don't think you understand, Miss Abbott."

"I don't think you understand, Mr. Lawyer. I've lost everything, and I can't deal with another one of Dirk's ploys." Why wouldn't this guy just go away? Having to face this now was close to torture.

He just kept talking as if she hadn't even ranted. "Mr. Miller has gifted you this facility. The building, the brand, the equipment, it's all yours to do with as you like, Miss Abbott." She glanced sharply at him and saw that he smiled happily as if he were her fairy godmother and Dirk really was Prince Charming. "Now if you'd like to read it over and sign, I can be on my way."

Kit blinked at him, slow to comprehend. Why would Dirk do this? She reiterated to the man, "He's giving me the gym?"

He nodded.

"Why?"

He shrugged. "You'd have to ask him that yourself, ma'am."

"Where is he?" she demanded, stepping closer to the man. Did Dirk think she'd be happy? Fall into his arms? Obviously, he didn't want her in his arms; he'd sent his lackey to bring her the news. To buy her off.

He backed up a step, and she wondered if she looked threatening. "I'm not sure, Miss Abbott. He was at the office this morning, but we don't see him very much."

"But someone there will know where he is?"

"I would suppose so. His father comes in every day."

"His father? He works for his father?"

"No, ma'am, Mr. Colin Miller owns the majority shares." He cleared his throat. "His father works for him, ma'am." His face showed that he was uncomfortable and not certain if he should be revealing so much. "Will you please sign?"

Kit absently looked over the documents. It appeared to be exactly what he was saying, but she didn't want to sign, not yet. She didn't know at this point if she would sign or throw them in Dirk's face. She clutched the papers. "I'll have my lawyer go over these and get them back to Mr. Miller."

The man straightened up. "I assure you, ma'am, everything is in order."

"I'm sure you're right, but I am going to return them to Mr. Miller personally. Now, is there an address for his building?"

He gestured to the papers. "It's on the document."

"Thank you." She hurried toward the door. He trailed her but didn't exit.

Kit rushed into her small office next to the entry and grabbed her purse, shoving the papers in it. The man stopped just outside the front door as she locked up.

"I'd really feel more comfortable keeping the papers in my possession."

"I'm sorry. Thanks for stopping by." Kit clutched the papers and hurried to her car. She glanced at the papers, telling Siri. "Navigate me to downtown Los Angeles."

"Six hours and twenty-nine minutes," Siri chirped back.

Yikes. She was in for a bit of a road trip. Kit didn't mind driving. It would give her time to process what Dirk was trying to do, gifting her the gym, and how she was going to proceed when she found him. She'd love to beat on his chest, maybe kiss him, and then throw his gift in his face and walk away like the strong woman she was. If only she knew how she'd react when she saw him again.

CHAPTER FOURTEEN

Colin flew back to L.A. from Boston on a chartered jet, not wanting to wait for one of his own to come pick him up. His assistant contacted Cavallo Point to have his things sent to his house on Malibu Colony Beach. He spent the night at the mansion he'd inherited from his grandfather. He was rarely here, but he liked the privacy and the views of the ocean. He spent a miserable Sunday not sure what to do with himself. He was tempted to walk into a church and find out more about the praying stuff Kit had shared with him, but he went on long walks on the beach, worked from home, and watched a couple of Marvel movies instead. Who knew Marvel movies had romance in them? He'd never noticed before.

He worked out from four to six a.m., Monday morning, before going into the office early, where he started plowing through work. There were several files in his inbox from the asset manager whose job it was to research small businesses to purchase. Colin itched to go through them and escape, but that was always his route: Escape. Instead he forced himself to stay planted behind his desk and work.

Once official work hours arrived, everyone from his secretary to his accounting team came by to say hello. He didn't get much work done, but it was great to see everyone. They all asked similar questions, "Where are you going? What are you buying next?" Colin had no answer for them. When his team of lawyers walked in, he did have an assignment and a ride on his Airbus for Brent, his most trusted legal representative. He sat staring out the windows of his high-rise office at the view of downtown L.A. wondering how Kit would take the news that he was giving the gym to her. It felt like the right thing to do.

He wondered if she really meant everything she'd said, especially that she couldn't trust him. He hadn't fully trusted her, had kept things from her, so he didn't blame her for not trusting him, for finally realizing he could never be worthy of her light and goodness. It still hurt though, but nothing hurt as bad as not being around her. She was sunshine and sparkle. He hadn't realized he was living in extreme darkness until he got to experience the light, and then it was hacked away from him. He passed a hand over his face and stood to stretch. Hacked away? Too many Marvel movies yesterday with Thor swinging his hammer.

A rap came on his door late in the afternoon. "Come in," he called, standing to greet the visitor. It seemed to be the day of distractions, but he was grateful his employees felt comfortable with him. It was better he didn't sit and stew about Kit.

His dad sauntered in, looking dapper as ever in a Brioni suit with his dark hair combed just so, and his blue eyes twinkling. "Son!"

He crossed the distance and hugged Colin as if they had a close relationship. Colin wondered if the farce was for his secretary just outside the door or the security guys who might glimpse it on the cameras.

He patted his dad awkwardly then stepped back, nodding a greeting.

"Sorry I'm so slow getting here to see you. Tracy and I had a tennis tournament this morning, and I didn't know you'd be in. But look at you. You look great." His eyes widened. "Something's happened to you." His dad stayed in his space, tilting his head and studying him.

Colin's stomach clenched. How could his dad know something had happened to him? He cleared his throat and said, "The latest property I purchased was the gym we discussed. I had the manager train me and she ..." he cleared his throat again, "was tough. Probably built some more muscle."

His dad's perceptive blue eyes ground into him. "You've always been in perfect health, son, it's not that."

Colin shrugged and stepped back, averting his gaze. "How've you been? How's Tracy?" He forced himself to try to be cordial, maybe it would get his dad out of his office without somehow prying out that Colin had fallen in love. How his dad would gloat then.

"Great. She's amazing. Son ..." He went and shut the door. Walking slowly back to the desk, he paused in front of Colin until he met his gaze. "She's helping me see some things, about me and you. You know ... our unresolved issues."

Oh, great. Just what he needed right now, hacking out emotional stuff with his dad. He needed to stop with the 'hacking' thoughts.

"What do you mean?" He met his dad's gaze evenly. "We're fine."

Thomas shook his head. "We're not fine. I've always blamed your mother for deserting us, and I let that warp my relationships with other women. But I recognize now that I also hurt you, damaged our relationship, because I didn't see how my problems, my lack of trust meant that you never had the opportunity to trust or love either. Not with me flitting through marriages like I did after ... Melanie."

His dad finally stopped. The air was thick and heavy. Had his dad really dared to go there? Melanie was the one subject neither of them touched, with good reason. The silence stretched, Colin could hardly meet his dad's gaze.

"I'm sorry," his dad continued when Colin said nothing. "I know you don't want to talk about this, but I have to say it." He cleared his throat, took a deep breath, and then rushed out, "Please forgive me, Colin. I love you, and I have been selfish and not put you first. Please, forgive me?"

Colin's throat was tight and scratchy. He tugged at his tie. This was not where he wanted to go with his dad, ever. "It's ... you're ... fine."

"It's not fine. I'm sorry." His dad skirted around the desk quickly and wrapped him up in another hug. Colin felt a strange and unfamiliar warmth rush through him. Well not completely unfamiliar, he'd felt a very different form of it when he touched Kit. Could he ... love his dad? He used to but he'd stifled any warmth for the man over the years. It just hurt too much. His dad had never taken responsibility for what he had done to Melanie, and Colin had hated him for it.

Something was different today. Colin found himself actually wrapping his arms around his dad's back and leaning into the hug. It felt awkward and healing. "I forgive you," he grunted out.

"Thank you, Colin, thank you." His dad sounded all choked up.

Surprised at this warmth that he felt, that he'd missed feeling from his dad, Colin pulled back from the hug and wondered at the grin on his dad's face. He beamed. He was lit up like Kit.

"You're really happy," Colin said.

"I am." His dad nodded. "Tracy takes me to this church every Sunday." He smiled. "I've found so much support and love. Yesterday, I even forgave myself for so many mistakes I've made over the years. And then to have you here today, to be able to ask you for forgiveness and hold you close. It's a sort of blessing they talk about at church, a weight removed from my heart." His eyes softened. "I love you, Colin. I'm so proud of you and the man you've become—military hero, successful businessman, and philanthropist. You're everything your mother or Melanie ever dreamed of you becoming, everything I ever dreamed you'd be."

Colin had to back away then. It was all sincere, and he knew his dad meant it, all of it, but it was too fast and too much for him. At the moment, he felt like he was nobody to brag about.

His dad patted his arm. "It's okay. I'll back off." He actually did back around the desk and sit down, leaning back like they were going to settle in for a great chat.

Colin stayed standing. He paced away to the windows, trying to catch his breath, processing all of these new ideas and feelings to know how to navigate around a father who still loved him as a hardened, grown man; despite all the times Colin tried to push him away. A father who was ... proud of him? He rubbed his palm over his chest, wondering at so many changes in his own heart.

"What happened with the gym in Sausalito?" his dad asked conversationally. "I heard the manager wasn't responding to your stipulations."

Colin glanced over his shoulder at his dad. He appeared genuinely interested, and it was obvious he was trying to change the subject, disperse the emotions, but he didn't realize the land mine he'd stepped into. What to say? "Well, Kit ..." His voice broke when he said her name. It was hard to say it and sound casual. "The manager, she's one of the most impressive people I've ever met." That was the understatement of the year. She was his world, and he'd walked away from her just like he'd feared he would. Why wasn't he chasing her down and fighting for her?

His dad's eyebrows rose, but he didn't comment.

"I gifted her the gym." The truth of what he'd done was out in the room before he could question why he'd want his dad to know the story.

His dad stood, his brow furrowed. "You've done many generous things with employees, but ... you gifted her everything?"

Colin nodded and turned away again. A few seconds passed, and then his dad snapped his fingers, his eyes widening in understanding. "Kit?"

Colin's stomach tumbled. *Kit.* He didn't turn around.

His dad intruded on his space, standing much too close to him at the windows. Excitement radiated off of his father. Finally, Colin glanced at him. He was a couple of inches taller than his dad and more filled out. He could easily push him away if he wanted to. "What?" Colin ground out.

His father smiled again. It was one of those smiles he used to give him as a teenager when Colin had done something and tried to hide it, but it was also a relieved, happy, and proud sort of smile. "You fell in love with her."

Colin's breath rushed out, and it was all he could do to not double over with the pain of losing her, or let the love he felt for Kit show in his face.

"Why else would you gift her the gym? It's written all over your face. Oh, Colin. I'm so happy. Finally, finally you found her." Then his dad was hugging him again.

All this hugging was too much. But how would his dad respond if he explained that, yes, he'd fallen in love, despite his best efforts to avoid it. He'd fallen in love, but she had to hate him for his deception, for trying to love her and fumbling it all up. He'd fallen in love, but she didn't trust him. That hurt as much as the idea of not ever seeing her again.

His dad pulled back, his blue eyes glistening.

Colin was the one marveling now. He hadn't seen his dad like this since Melanie. "What has Tracy done to you?"

He laughed. "Loved me. She truly loves me, despite what a mess I am. Does your Kit truly love you?"

Colin backed away, shaking his head. Kit's love had been pure and beautiful. He'd tainted it by not trusting her enough to tell her everything before she found out from someone else. "She did. I messed it up."

His dad smiled his understanding. "We Miller men are experts at that. But you love her?"

Colin nodded miserably. *Love.*

"Well then, go to her, beg her to take you back and then show her every minute how much you love her. It's worth it."

Colin couldn't believe he would consider advice from his father, who'd been through more women than businesses Colin had acquired.

"I know that look. You think I'm a philandering piece of work, but I've only truly loved three women—your mom, Melanie, and now, Tracy. I realize now that every time it has truly been love, not a cheap imitation, it has been worth any pain I experienced, any sacrifice. Go to her, please. Don't wait until you're my age to figure it out."

Colin swallowed hard. His heart raced at the thought of chasing after Kit. She'd be back in Sausalito. Would she turn him away? Would the warmth in her blue eyes have disappeared? Would fireworks happen if only he could touch her again?

He'd revealed too much earlier in the conversation and let too much time pass right now to pretend nonchalance, but he tried anyway. He was emotionally spent. "Thanks, Dad, I'll think about it." He forced himself to sit at his desk and click on his computer.

His dad didn't move. When Colin finally glanced up, his dad was glowering at him. "Go to her, or you'll regret it forever, like I regret turning my back on Melanie."

Colin didn't appreciate him bringing up Melanie again, but he heard himself asking what he'd always stewed about, but never voiced, "Why did you turn your back on Melanie?"

A few beats passed before his dad sighed, and then said simply, "She cheated on me." Only four words but they were wrought with emotion.

"What?" Colin sprang to his feet. He couldn't have heard him right. Melanie would never, but if she had, he could understand his dad flipping out and divorcing her. His dad had a strict moral code about cheating. Through all of his marriages, Thomas Miller had never cheated, had always followed proper protocols of divorce and marital vows, never overlapping the two.

"We were going through some hard times. I was being selfish and too focused on work, golf, trying to be there for your grandfather in his last few months, and a hundred other things. She was working with a personal trainer daily, trying to be perfect to get my attention. She and the trainer got close, became good friends." He shook his head and muttered, "Very good friends."

Colin had no idea what to say, how to process this.

Studying his hands for a few seconds his dad admitted, "I blame myself. She was lonely, and I was stupid and selfish, but when she told me she'd been ... intimate and thought she was falling in love with him..." He passed a hand over his face. "I went nuts. For me it was your mother ditching me all over again. Melanie and I tried to work it out, for you. She truly loved you, son, but you were an adult and deployed, so she could justify that you didn't need her anymore. She wanted to be with him and finally asked me for the divorce. Then I guess she felt such guilt that she ... well, you know what happened in the end."

"Why didn't you tell me any of this?" Colin clung to his chair. He hated that Melanie had done that, but he knew his dad was right, she had at least loved him. She had always put him first, proven that she loved him as if he were her own child. Yet she'd betrayed his dad, and then died, leaving Colin as surely as his mom had.

"You were busy with the Navy, and I knew you needed stability, not another woman deserting you. I decided I wanted to take full blame, especially after she died."

Colin rushed around the desk, and now he was the one claiming a hug. His dad hugged him back fiercely. "I'm sorry, Dad. I blamed you and hated you. All this time ... you took my anger and never threw it back at me. I'm so sorry."

"It's okay, son. I wanted to be strong for you. I did plenty of selfish things that were worthy of your blame over the years."

"Nobody's perfect."

His dad chuckled.

They pulled back and stared at each other. It was still a little awkward, all this hugging and emotional talk, but it felt good. His dad patted Colin's arm and grinned. "You've got some place to go. Come see us when you get back. I want to meet this Kit."

With that, his dad finally walked out the office door, shutting it behind him. Colin didn't want to see him go and that alone was a startling change. He pulled his phone up and clicked on one of his standby pilot's numbers. Should he do it? Fly to Sausalito? Beg Kit to forgive him? He sank into his desk chair, still processing everything that had happened with his dad. He didn't know that he could handle much more emotional overload today, but for Kit ... He would do anything.

CHAPTER FIFTEEN

K it's eyes were gritty. Her neck ached as she navigated through L.A. traffic at four p.m. "I thought rush hour was at five," she murmured. Apparently, nobody had informed the people here that they were supposed to work until five, and then battle to get home.

She'd hurried home from the gym this morning to change and make sure she was looking good, not puffy from crying over him. She had to show Dirk she was in control, that he had no power over her ... if only that were true.

She'd made good time cruising down the I-5. The sunny, summer weather would have been beautiful for a day of driving, if she hadn't been so stirred up. What was she doing, chasing after Dirk? Was it only to tell him she didn't want to be bought off by accepting his gift of 'her' gym? Or was she hoping he'd fall to his knees, confess his love, and they'd have a chance? They didn't have a chance. She felt betrayed, and he probably lumped her in with the other women who'd deserted him. Still, there was something in her that wanted that confrontation, answers to more questions, the chance to say goodbye, and some closure.

But now she was stuck, two blocks from Dirk's office, according to Siri. Horns honked around her. Kit needed to use the restroom, and she was going to miss Dirk, if he left at five. If he was even at his office. How would she find him then? Miserable. That's what she was right now.

A car pulled out of a metered parking space. Kit put on her blinker and darted into the spot. She could run much faster than this traffic was moving. Grabbing her purse, she used a credit card in the meter, and then jogged along the sidewalk, darting through pedestrians. Not an easy feat in these heels, but she was on a mission.

The warm summer sun made her hot and sticky, and she needed a restroom worse than ever when she burst into the building she hoped was Dirk's. A smiling receptionist greeted her. "Miller International?" Kit gasped out.

"Fifteenth floor."

"Thank you." She hurried for the elevator but diverted to the ladies' room. Hurrying to use it and freshen up herself and her makeup the best she could, she straightened her fitted, teal blue dress and took a steadying breath. It was time to find him and ... who knew what would happen then? Maybe he hated her for sending him away in Boston? Maybe he thought the gift of the gym was a nice parting gesture for what they'd shared? Maybe he'd actually meant it when he told Lottie he loved her? She pushed out a breath and said a prayer for strength and discernment.

The elevator ascended quickly and before she knew it, she was standing in the lobby of a spacious business office that was obviously important and high-end. A logo with Miller International was splayed on the wall behind a reception desk. Dirk owned Miller International. She was still trying to wrap her head around the truth of who Dirk really was. Colin Miller. He was a successful, powerful billionaire. She'd seen first-hand how cold and unemotional he could be. She gulped. This had the makings of disaster. What was she doing coming here? A personal trainer from a tiny town braving a meeting with a powerful king in his own throne room, what did she expect to happen next?

More timidly than she'd ever felt in her life, she approached the desk. A beautiful redhead smiled up at her. "May I help you?"

"I'm here to see Dirk Miller."

The lady's brow squiggled. "*Dirk* Miller?"

"Oh! Excuse me, I mean Colin." Colin, not her Dirk. Logically she knew that, but emotionally, it was rough to comprehend.

"Do you have an appointment?"

"No, but I'm his ... employee, of sorts." She was making no sense, but her palms were sweaty, and her tongue felt thick.

The lady eyed her strangely but nodded. "Let me see if Mr. Miller can meet with you."

"Thank you." Kit stayed planted right in front of the desk.

The lady pressed a button on her phone and waited and waited.

Finally, she glanced up at her. "I'm sorry. It appears Mr. Miller has gone for the day. Can I leave a message?"

Kit felt like she'd taken a fist to the abdomen. No matter if she admitted it to herself, or not, she wanted Dirk or at least the chance to get some closure with him. He was gone. How would she find him? What would she do? She had classes in the morning and didn't want to leave her people high and dry, but she wanted to plop down and wait until Dirk appeared.

She didn't know how to respond as the lady stared expectantly at her. Suddenly, a tall, dark-haired man walked around the reception wall.

"Dirk?" Kit murmured, but it wasn't Dirk. This man wasn't as tall or broad, and there were lines in his face and gray in his hair that Dirk didn't have, but he could've been his ... father.

The man smiled a greeting to her. "Can I help you?"

"Dirk," she repeated dumbly.

His blue eyes, that were so like his son's, were warm on her face. But this was the man who had messed Dirk up. How could he look so kind and friendly? "Are you ... Kit?" he asked.

She nodded.

He chuckled, and his eyes got even more sparkly. "You came for him."

"Um, no ... sort of." She didn't know what to say to this man, what to share. He put off an aura of confidence, kindness, and faith. After the stress of the past couple of days, she was tempted to go hug him, but she knew how he was with women, how he'd damaged Dirk, so she held back. If Dirk hadn't been so damaged by his parents maybe they would've had a chance.

He approached her and stuck out his hand. "Thomas Miller. It's a pleasure to meet you, Kit."

She shook his hand, feeling out of sorts and awkward, not herself at all.

"You've just missed him." Thomas directed her back toward the elevator.

"Where was he going?" she managed to get out.

"To find you."

The room swayed. He'd gone to find her. Why had he sent his lawyer this morning only to try himself now? Nothing made sense to her, least of all her own feelings.

Thomas studied her. When she didn't say anything, he continued, "My son didn't tell me everything that transpired between you, but I've never seen my boy lit up, and yet miserable, like he was today. He loves you. The question is, how do you feel about him?"

"I love him," she admitted. "But ... I'm mad at him, too, and ... it's all messed up!"

Thomas threw his head back and laughed, "He told me he messed it all up."

"He did." She swallowed and admitted, "But maybe I did too."

He appraised her for a few seconds then said, "You may have heard that I've been through a few relationships."

Kit arched her eyebrows, having no response to that.

"If I've learned anything it's that we all make mistakes, but love is worth working through them. Please give my son a chance."

Kit wanted to give Dirk that chance. It swelled in her, but she still didn't know if she could trust him or his dad. Pulling the contract of purchase out of her purse, she held it up. "What did he mean by this? Was he just trying to buy me off?"

His dad smiled softly. "He was trying to tell you he loved you. My son has a giving heart, he's done a lot of kind things for his employees, but he has never, ever gifted one of them a business."

Kit mulled this over. She didn't know Dirk as well as she wanted, but she could feel the truth of what his dad was saying. Could Dirk truly love her like his father thought?

"It's yours, Kit. Sign it and know it's a gift, no strings attached." His smile grew. "But if you love my son, please, let's stop wasting time and go find him."

Kit liked him. Despite the fact that she shouldn't like him on principle, of standing up for Dirk with how this man had damaged him, she couldn't seem to help herself. Dirk's dad was humble, and he obviously loved Dirk. She wasn't a hundred percent certain that she and Dirk had a chance or that their love that developed so quickly wouldn't just burn out like Dirk had feared, but she suddenly wanted to try, more than anything.

Shoving the papers back into her purse she realized they were the catalyst that got her to come, but the gym was the least of her concerns at the moment. Dirk. She wanted to give him a chance. "Can we catch him?"

Thomas grinned and punched a fist in the air. "Yes! Let's go." His smile slid a little bit. "Shoot. Hang this traffic. He'll get to the airport first. Let's call him."

"No. Please. I need to see him." Whatever happened between them she wanted it to happen in person, and she needed to see him.

"I have an idea." He pulled out his phone, dialed a number and spoke rapidly, something about favors and a helicopter. A helicopter? Kit's nerves ramped up. She'd never flown in a helicopter. It sounded exciting, but all she cared about was getting to Dirk and resolving things between them. Thomas was right— she needed to at least give Dirk a chance.

Thomas hung up, said goodbye to the receptionist, and escorted Kit into the elevator. He grinned at her as they ascended to the roof. "You love my Colin."

Kit didn't quite know how to respond to that, but she wanted to know. "Forgive me for saying this, but ... he kind of painted you as the bad guy."

Thomas's lips tightened, but he nodded easily. "He was right, but I love my boy and would do anything for him."

"I'm glad to hear that."

"I'm just glad you're here."

They stood there smiling awkwardly at each other, their current and future relationship still a little uncertain, hinging on how Dirk responded to Kit when they found him. *Please let him love me*, she prayed fervently. Finally the doors to the elevator opened. It was hot and windy on the rooftop. They only waited a few minutes before the whir of helicopter blades sounded, and then a small helicopter appeared and landed on the circular H spot on the roof. It was just like the movies as Kit clung to her hair and her dress while Thomas ushered her across the roof and helped her into the helicopter. It was too loud to talk, but she waved hello to the pilot who grinned at her.

Dirk's dad shut the door, settled into the seat by the pilot, and put a headset on. Kit strapped on a seatbelt and watched out the window, excitement thrumming through her as they lifted off and soared over L.A. Buildings and traffic flowed underneath her, the ocean off to her left. The ride was incredible, but the fact that Dirk's dad was taking her to him was the cause of most of her excitement and nerves. His dad said his son was all lit up and loved Kit. Was it true or simply a father hoping for his son to be happy?

They landed at a small airport, thanked the pilot, and climbed out. Thomas held on to Kit's elbow as they rushed through a tiny terminal and onto another tarmac. He pointed. "That's Colin's Airbus."

Colin's Airbus. She was in another world, and it was still hard to wrap her mind around Dirk not being a waiter, not even being Dirk. The plane looked deserted. They rushed up to it and Thomas hurried up the open stairs and was back within a few seconds. "He's not here yet. The stewardess is prepping the plane, and the pilot is in filing flight plans. Plans to get him to you." He grinned.

Kit's heart was pumping hard. They'd beat Dirk here. So now she had to wait. Waiting was the last thing she wanted to do.

"Why don't you come into the plane and get out of the sun?" Thomas suggested.

At that moment a black Escalade pulled up in the parking lot adjacent to the tarmac, and a man climbed out of the backseat. He looked handsome, powerful, successful, and irresistible in a tailored suit with his dark hair perfectly combed and his blue eyes focusing immediately on her.

"Dirk!" It ripped out of Kit's lungs. Any doubts, frustrations, or fears she had disappeared the moment she saw him. This was the man for her, and she'd known it from that moment they touched by the waterfall. It was crazy. It was fast. It was incredible. She loved Dirk Colin Miller, and they could work out anything they needed to; they could add kindling, sticks, logs, maybe even starter fluid if needed, to keep their fire burning bright.

She ran at him, praying she wouldn't trip in her heels. He was so close, but too far away. She wanted to be in his arms and be there now.

Dirk's face broke into a relieved grin, and he ran toward her. His smile and perfect face grew closer. She wanted to tell him everything she was thinking and feeling, after she kissed him for hours.

She reached him and flung her arms around his neck and her body against him. He swept her off the ground and swung her around. "Kit!"

Setting her feet down, he held her tightly against him. "You came for me?"

"I was wrong. I'm sorry. Sorry I sent you away in Boston. Sorry I didn't let you explain."

"It's okay. You came for me."

She smiled. "I love you, Dirk. No matter what you did or didn't tell me. I love you."

"I love you." Dirk's gaze travelled over her, savoring her, taking her in. "There are so many things I need to tell you, to apologize for. I was so wrong, and I love you so much."

"You can apologize later," she said. "You have things to do right now."

"Oh?" His handsome face split into a wide grin. "What should I be doing right now?"

"Kissing me."

He chuckled, but he didn't waste time as he bent his head and claimed her lips. This kiss was more powerful than anything she'd experienced. The physical connection was amazing, but they loved each other and that was even more miraculous for two people who hadn't planned on finding this kind of love.

Clapping and hoots came from behind them. They broke apart and Dirk glanced over. "I see you met my dad."

"Yeah, he's great."

"He is. I was ... wrong about him too. I was wrong about a lot of things, Kit. Most of all, I was wrong to not trust you with everything. You loved me, and I was too scared to share the truth about me, too scared you wouldn't want the real me."

Thomas approached and hugged them both at once. "Sorry to interrupt. Just an old man that's so happy." He patted them each on the shoulder, backed away, and saluted them. "I'll let you have your moment. Come see us soon, please."

"We will," Dirk promised.

"I love you, son. Nice to meet you, Kit." He turned and jogged across the tarmac.

Kit smiled at the interaction but focused back on Dirk. "I want you, Dirk... Colin... whoever you are. I love every bit of you, the good and the bad. I'm *never* going to walk away from any part of you."

Dirk's blue eyes brightened, and he hugged her tightly. He softly kissed her and murmured, "I promise to be there for you and love every bit of you too. Lucky for me there is no bad in you."

Kit laughed. "Oh, just you wait. I've got a temper that you won't believe."

He chuckled. "I did see a little of that when I ticked you off, repeatedly."

"Well then, just behave yourself."

Dirk slid his hands up her back, making tingles erupt. He took his time, running his hands across her neck, cradling her face with his palms, and staring at her with his beautiful, blue eyes. "I love you, Kit."

"I love you, Dirk."

"I don't care if you call me Dirk or jerk or Prince Charming," he winked, "but I've been having these visions of you kissing me and calling me Colin."

Kit smiled slowly and said, "I can make your visions come true." Her body filled with warmth as she kissed him, and then murmured against his lips, "I love you ... Colin."

Colin grinned against her mouth and proceeded to kiss her again. She lost track of time and all rational thought, but it didn't matter. She was in Dirk-Colin's arms, and that was the spot where she was meant to be.

EPILOGUE

The view from their suite at Oracle Park was incredible, overlooking the bay. Kit had come to a few San Francisco Giants' games with her family, but they'd never had a suite.

Colin was talking with some of his employees, beaming. He caught her gaze on him, excused himself, and hurried to her side.

"Don't do that again," he murmured, leaning in and kissing her.

"Go to the restroom?"

"Yeah, I don't like being away from you."

Kit laughed. "Oh, you are a silly man. I hate being away from you, too." She lowered her voice and whispered, "Colin." Then she kissed him.

Colin hugged her tight. "I wish we were alone right now."

"You always want me alone." She winked and cast a glance

around at everyone staring at them. "Are they in shock that the great Colin Miller is smitten by a woman?"

"Probably, but they're actually staring at us for a different reason." He pointed out the open suite windows at the Jumbotron. Kit and Colin were the focus. Across the live video feed of them were the words, "Kit ... will you marry me?"

Kit's stomach swooped. Her gaze darted back to Colin. His blue eyes were warm on her, and a little bit uncertain. He dropped to one knee and clasped her hand. "I know it's too quick, but I've got so much kindling and logs stored up for you. I won't ever let us burn out."

Kit squeezed his hand, tears pricking at her eyes. "I know you won't."

"I love you, Katherine Shelley Abbott."

Kit smiled, wondering if her mom or Mae had told him her full name.

"Marry me, please?" With his free hand, he pulled a sparkling, square-cut diamond ring out of his shirt pocket.

"That thing is massive," Kit said.

Colin chuckled and stood, pulling her close. "Please say yes, love?"

Kit kissed him, and then shouted, "Yes!" The stadium broke into applause. Kit laughed but ignored everyone around them as Colin slid the diamond ring on her finger and kissed her again. This fire was a quick burn, but it was a lasting burn as well.

Their love wouldn't burn out. Oh, how she loved Dirk Colin Johanson Miller.

———————

I hope you loved Kit and Dirk's story. If you missed Mae and Slade's romance of mistake identities and funny t-shirts, find *Her Dream Date Boss* here.

ABOUT THE AUTHOR

Cami is a part-time author, part-time exercise consultant, part-time housekeeper, full-time wife, and overtime mother of four adorable boys. Sleep and relaxation are fond memories. She's never been happier.

Join Cami's VIP list to find out about special deals, giveaways and new releases and receive a free copy of *Rescued by Love: Park City Firefighter Romance* by clicking here.

Read on for a short excerpt of Mae and Slade's story, *Her Dream Date Boss*. Happy reading!

cami@camichecketts.com
www.camichecketts.com

HER DREAM DATE BOSS

Mae Delaney refastened her long, dark hair into its standard ponytail, pushed her large glasses firmly into place, smoothed down one of her favorite T-shirts, and made sure the screen angle didn't show she was in yoga pants at two p.m. She ran some pineapple lip gloss over her lips and practiced her smile in the mirror. "Look at you, you stinking hottie. You're going to slaughter him." The self-talk helped a tiny bit. She was the furthest thing from hot, and her thick glasses made it impossible to see her dark eyes, which her best friend, Kit, reassured her were her best feature.

Her stomach fluttering, she pushed the button on video chat to call Slade Steele: the most charming and handsome man on the planet, owner of Steele Wholesale Lending, and her boss.

Slade's perfectly sculpted face filled the screen, complemented by his deep brown eyes with lashes longer than her own and a trimmed beard that only served to highlight his intriguing lips.

He was gorgeous but so down-to-earth and kind. She scoured the internet nightly for Slade Steele sightings. Over the last few months, she'd seen him on humanitarian trips with his church, helping a child who'd lost his mom at a hockey game, taking his beautiful little sister who had Down syndrome to the premiere of a chick flick, and playing rugby with teenage boys at the park. In one of the rugby pictures, he'd had his shirt off. She sighed inadvertently.

"Hi, Mae. How are you today?"

"If I was any better, I'd be exalted already," she said.

He chuckled. "Well, lucky for me, you're still on this planet."

"Lucky, lucky you. Do you ever stop and thank the good Lord that you get the blessing of talking to me most days of the week?"

He grinned. "Yes, ma'am, I do." His eyes trailed over her T-shirt, and he read it out loud. "People in sleeping bags ... are the soft tacos of the bear world." Chuckling, he said, "Does that mean you have an aversion to tacos?"

"No, sir. I like tacos. I just don't want to be a taco."

He grinned. "Good to know."

All of Mae's nerves settled, replaced with a deep longing to track him down, throw herself against his well-formed chest, kiss him good and long, and tell him she'd loved him for almost two years now. Then maybe they could go for tacos. But thinking about his well-formed chest ... Could she touch it at their first meeting, or would that be an inappropriate action for a good Christian girl? She'd never really dated, so she had no idea. Hmm. It might be worth it. She might not get exalted as quickly, but she could repent later.

"Mae. Mae?"

"What? What just happened? Is it hot in here?" She fanned her face.

Slade laughed. "I'm not sure what your weather is like in Sausalito, so I have no idea. It's steamy hot in Boston."

Steamy hot? Oh, my. She wanted him to say those words again. Even better, maybe he could say them after they kissed the first time. *Focus, Mae.* "Dang man reminding me of the sad state of my life."

"What's that?"

"Never being where you are."

Slade's cheek twitched as if he was holding back laughter. "Can we get back to that state in a moment? I need some help from my best account rep."

"Of course you do. It's the only reason you ever call me." Of course he'd never call her for any reason but work. He was the perfect male model who dated the perfect female models. He lived in a different world than she did. At least she had these short conversations most days of the week, and she could dream of him.

"Must I remind you that you called me?" He winked, and Mae had to fan herself again.

"Stop flirting with me and tell me what the problem is."

Slade smiled, probably thinking he'd never flirt with the likes of her, but he was too classy to say that. He began listing for her which branches were having issues she needed to resolve. She was the liaison between his lending companies and the local mortgage companies. Mae typed away into her computer as he spoke.

"You know you could email me most of this?" Mae said, though she immediately regretted it.

"Don't say that. Then I would miss out on my daily dose of Mae humor."

"I'm actually funnier with my fingertips."

He blinked at her. "Hmm. Maybe I'll try email tomorrow."

"Please don't. I like seeing your handsome face." Her neck was burning, and she prayed that he wouldn't call her out or fire her for inappropriate talking in the workplace. But she worked remotely and he was the owner, so hopefully her blatant flirtations were okay.

"You're the one that suggested email."

"Forgive me. My brain vacates its lovely home when I stare into those deep brown eyes."

"Ah, Mae." He gifted her with his earth-moving smile. "You're good for the self-esteem. Hey, I've gotta run. I'm actually flying into San Francisco in a few hours. Do you want to get together for lunch or dinner tomorrow? I'll come across the bay to Sausalito."

Mae froze. Her stomach was swirling like it was full of butterflies, and her mouth and throat were so dry she couldn't even swallow. Slade Steele was coming to San Francisco, and he wanted to go to lunch or dinner with her?

Oh my goodness! Oh my goodness!

What should she do? Her brain whirled—play it cool, get a drink of water, find a firefighter to drench her with his hose, or call her sassy best friend Kit and have her come answer him? That would take too long, though, and he was staring at her, awaiting her answer. Mae tried to squeak out a yes, but nothing came out.

"Maybe not the best idea?" Slade asked, his dark eyes filling with concern.

If Mae missed this opportunity, Kit would sentence her to a year of walking lunges or some other exercise torture. Kit forced her to attend her boot camp class each morning, and it never got easier for Mae.

Slade waited, one perfect eyebrow arched up. "It's all right, Mae—"

"I'll go to dinner with you!" she yelled. "Yes!" Hallelujah. Praise every saintly ancestor she didn't even know and her beloved family watching from up above. She'd finally found her tongue and answered affirmatively, if a bit too eagerly.

Keep reading *Her Dream Date Boss* here.

ALSO BY CAMI CHECKETTS

Steele Family Romance

Her Dream Date Boss

Quinn Family Romance

The Devoted Groom

The Conflicted Warrior

The Gentle Patriot

The Tough Warrior

Her Too-Perfect Boss

Her Forbidden Bodyguard

Hawk Brothers Romance

The Determined Groom

The Stealth Warrior

Her Billionaire Boss Fake Fiance

Risking it All

Navy Seal Romance

The Protective Warrior

The Captivating Warrior

The Stealth Warrior

Texas Titan Romance

The Fearless Groom

The Trustworthy Groom

Christmas Makeover

Last of the Gentlemen

My Best Man's Wedding

Change of Plans

Counterfeit Date

Snow Valley

Full Court Devotion: Christmas in Snow Valley

A Touch of Love: Summer in Snow Valley

Running from the Cowboy: Spring in Snow Valley

Light in Your Eyes: Winter in Snow Valley

Romancing the Singer: Return to Snow Valley

Fighting for Love: Return to Snow Valley

Other Books by Cami

The Loyal Patriot: Georgia Patriots Romance

Seeking Mr. Debonair: Jane Austen Pact

Seeking Mr. Dependable: Jane Austen Pact

Saving Sycamore Bay

How to Design Love

Oh, Come On, Be Faithful

Protect This

Blog This

Redeem This

The Broken Path

Dead Running

Dying to Run

Fourth of July

Love & Loss

Love & Lies

Cami's Collections

Hawk Brothers Romance Collection

Cami's Military Collection

Billionaire Beach Romance Collection

Billionaire Bride Pact Collection

Billionaire Romance Sampler

Echo Ridge Romance Collection

Texas Titans Romance Collection

Snow Valley Collection

Christmas Romance Collection

Made in the USA
San Bernardino, CA
04 March 2020

65316749R00106